# A SHADOW IN THE LIGHT

Parallel Verse Guardians - Book One

## KEARY TAYLOR

## RESURRECTING MAGIC SERIES

Rise of the Mage

Keeper of the Lost

Shadow of the Locked

Academy of the Found

## THE BLOOD DESCENDANTS UNIVERSE

### House of Royals Saga

House of Royals

House of Pawns

House of Kings

House of Judges

House of Ravens

### Garden of Thorns Trilogy

Garden of Thorns

Garden of Snakes

Garden of Graves

### Crown of Death Saga

Crown of Death

Crown of Blood

Crown of Ruin

Crown of Bones

## THE FALL OF ANGELS TRILOGY

Branded

Forsaken

Vindicated

Afterlife (the novelette companion to Vindicated)

Returned (ten year anniversary follow up)

## THE EDEN TRILOGY

The Raid (An Eden Short Story)

The Ashes (an Eden Prequel)

The Bane (Book 1)

The Human (Book 2)

The Eve (Book 3)

## THE NERON RISING SAGA

Neron Rising

Neron Skies

Nero Awakening

Nero Blood

Nero Nights

Neron Wars

Nero Kingdom

Chapter One

_______________

"CAN YOU CONFIRM?"

Davorian's voice cuts through the room with the sharpness of a knife.

There's a full twenty seconds of silence, save for the sound of feet crossing broken glass scattered across gravel coming through the speaker of the phone.

"Confirmed," she says. "Agent Calista is dead."

A collective curse slips from every set of lips in the room. For ten seconds, no one says anything.

Another one down. Another one terminated. We're slowly getting picked off, one by one. And soon, there will be none of us left.

"Get out of there, Agent Cordelia," Davorian says. "I want you out of the area for twenty-four hours, at least."

"Affirmative," Cordelia says on the other end, and she cuts the com.

I look up as my stomach turns over. Every face around me is grim. Just as torn apart as I am.

There are only six of us here. Where once we were a strong army, we've been scattered throughout the world out of necessity. And now, we're disappearing off the face of this planet, one at a time.

"We're never going home," I say. The words just slip from my brain to my lips, but I mean them. After all this time, after fighting this hard, we have to accept it.

"Don't say that," Ascelin says, his voice dark and harsh, sharpened by grief.

My eyes rise to meet his. He's angry at me for saying the words. It's all we've worked for; all we've fought for. He still hopes.

"It's been this long," I say, my words a tired whisper. "There are only this many of us left. It's time to accept it. We're stuck here."

"We're all hurting, Serena," Philomena says as she fixes me with her dark eyes. "Don't make things worse."

*Please shut up*, that's what she's politely saying.

I get up from my seat at the conference table, which is kind of a joke considering there are only six of us and there are seats here for eighteen. I head for the door, stepping out into the main passageway.

"Where are you going?" Renwick asks with an impatient sigh.

"Out," I say without looking back. "Might as well go enjoy this life I'm stuck with forever."

I know I'm being immature. I know I'm being childish. I know Philomena is right, and I'm making this worse for everyone, because I know it is hard on everyone.

But I'm just so tired. I'm just too burned out.

I need out. I need to not live this life for a while.

The compound is deep underground, far enough below the surface we escape the heat. It's huge, really, if you consider how many people it now houses. Once upon a time, we built it to shelter over five hundred of us. Not comfortably, but under desperate circumstances, we could all come down here and we'd be safe. It had been difficult, because back then, there weren't the modern tools they have now. It had been our bare hands and rudimentary tools.

Rooms branch off the main hall, leading to offices and bedrooms. Davorian's, the director. Nisha's, the assignment director. Ascelin's, the head of security, now essentially a one-man team. And one for each of us agents: me, Renwick, and Philomena.

There's a massive bunkroom, with beds to sleep the small army we once were. There's a massive kitchen, and bathrooms with plumbing that has been updated throughout the years.

But here in the center, in the heart, there is a railing. I stop at it, my hands wrapping around the cold steel, and my eyes slide down into the dark.

A beautiful swirl of red and gold and white sandstone spirals down. And at the bottom, shadows swirl and float, lazy and dark and haunting. It's like a living thing, calling and teasing.

It's the way home.

It's right there.

But without the key, we can't open it.

We can't go back.

My stomach knots and I push away from the rail, aiming back down the hall, feeling eyes on me as I walk away.

It's dark down here. There's not a single light, only those cast secondarily from electronics, sharp cuts of red or green. But I don't struggle to find my way. I can see perfectly, better than I can on the surface.

Two hundred yards. That's how long the main passage stretches. And at the end, I reach a tunnel.

A sandstone tube rises above my head. It twists and turns, a variance of fifteen feet or so. I can barely see the hue of light somewhere up above.

It's as natural as breathing.

I let a breath out, and I release the shadows inside of me.

Black pincers and willowy legs spring from me. My body loses its shape, growing and shifting. Swirls of shadow slip out of me. I feel the bones in my face change shape, elongating, fangs growing in my mouth. No longer two legs but a dozen, long and skinny and deadly.

I reach out, bracing one leg against the tube, and then three others.

I begin my climb up and up, the effort easy and quick in my darkling form.

In this world, they would say I am ugly. A thing of nightmares. Not a spider, not a beast. I am a shadow insect monster.

But this is the form I was born to take.

This is my power. My gift. This is what I was given to protect my world.

Specks of sand break off and fall down through the tunnel. It has widened slowly over time, scraped away by hundreds of sets of pincers and spindly legs.

The sky is just starting to darken when I reach the opening—a cut in the red rocks, tucked between two boulders. It's invisible unless you know it's there, just a shadow of an indent.

I shift back to my natural form when I step from the entrance, smoothing my shirt, pulling the collar of my jacket straight.

The motorcycle is hidden between some other rocks. I pull the key from my pocket and straddle the machine, inserting the key and revving it to life.

Through the fading light, I rip over the rocks.

We're hidden well. There's a lot of desert in Nevada. Few tourists come this way. These aren't the most famous red rocks in the area. People go to Utah for that, or the Grand Canyon. But there are some hikers, the occasional hard-core enthusiast.

In all the time we've been here, we've never once had an issue.

Not that we're counting on it staying that way. There's a reason Ascelin has his title. We have security in place in case of an incident.

I rip along the dirt road when I reach it. All the way down to the highway, and then along its smooth surface. The glow of the city is bright, even this time of day where the sun is just starting to think about slipping below the horizon. They call Paris the city of lights, but I have to really wonder which is brighter? It, or Las Vegas?

It's a Friday night, which means the city is going to be insane. And the middle of July, so it's unbearably hot. This is the desert, so we do cool down, but considering the 110-degree peaks, it takes a while.

I crank the gas harder, bulleting through the fading light, aiming for my apartment.

My building is a whole block and a half east of The Strip. It's a tan colored building, five stories high, occupied by dozens of people who work in Sin City. Full of waitresses, strippers, cooks, housekeepers, all twenty-something-year-olds, just like me.

I pull into my one covered parking spot, tucking myself up as close to the curb as I can, just in front of my black car.

Black is such a terrible choice when you live in the desert of Nevada. But when it's your favorite color…

I climb the stairs, all the way up to the fifth floor and unlock my door.

The AC is blasting, making that horrible rattling noise. I set my keys in the dish by the door. I cross to the kitchenette, grabbing anything I can find. An apple and a leftover quesadilla.

All these years, and I still can't get over the food. The one and only thing I find better about this side. Their food is out of this world.

Going to the closet, I flip through my limited choices. I work. All the time. I work in the dark and I have to remain hidden most of the time. My wardrobe is almost entirely black.

Except for one impulse purchase toward the back. A little red dress.

I slip into it, and it hugs all my curves in the right ways. It enhances my bust, giving me a mile of confidence. I don some black shoes and step into the bathroom.

Anyone looking at me wouldn't see anything to be concerned about. According to their standards, I'm pretty. Big brown eyes. Long dark brown hair. Full lips. A slender, fit frame.

Too bad they wouldn't like the other side of me.

I dig through my makeup, applying darker eye shadow and mascara. My hair is a little wild. Naturally, it holds a loose curl. It's a little windswept after riding from the compound to here. I run my fingers through it, getting it to look a little more tamed.

It's not perfect. But it's exactly how I feel tonight. I feel like a mess. I feel angry. I feel reckless and maybe a little stupid.

I don't want to be me tonight.

I want to forget who I am and that I don't belong here.

I tuck my phone, my fake ID, and some money into my dress. And I step out of my apartment, locking it, and head down the stairs.

"You working tonight?"

I pause before going down the third floor. Tim, a guy who works as an acrobat, leans over his railing from the fourth floor, looking down at me.

"Not tonight," I say, giving him just a tiny smile. "Tonight, I'm going to be someone else."

He looks at me, not sure how to take what I've said. It's out of character. And I've never smiled at him.

"You're going out by yourself?" he asks, worry obvious in his tone.

I smile, entertained by his worry. "I'll be okay."

"Be careful," he says. "Call me if you get in any trouble."

I nod appreciatively, but don't say anything as I turn and continue down the stairs.

Being pretty is annoying sometimes. Guys think they have a shot or that they have an obligation to try, just because you're pretty, and even more so if they're pretty, too.

But Tim really is a nice guy.

I can't complain too much, though. It does make my life easier most of the time. Hate me for it or not, it's a fact, and I'll use it to my advantage when it suits what I need.

The sidewalk is already crowded, filling with people, even locals headed out for a night of fun. A night of mistakes and memories. I slip into the crowd, blending right in. No one would even realize I was going out for a night on The Strip alone, there are so many bodies out.

The sun might be down now, but it's still so hot. Why, of all places, did the gate have to be in the desert, where no human should be able to survive? Where I'm from, we stick to the cooler weather, where there's actually water and a chance of surviving should the power go out.

These people and their sunshine.

I certainly have different places I avoid. After being stuck in Las Vegas for so long, I've visited every place there is. I probably know Vegas better than anyone alive, so I know the places that will eat you alive, get you raped, get you killed, or make you disappear altogether.

But I don't have any particular places I love. There's expensive, impressive, good, and better.

I wander with the crowd for a bit, turning my face up to the sky. I listen to all the sounds around me. The people talking excitedly, the buskers, the hecklers who want my money. I take in the lights, the traffic fighting to make its way through the crowd.

I certainly feel alive here. I feel human here. I like the feeling that I can fit in and get lost and that for just one night, I can be like everyone else.

When the crowd gets so thick I can no longer push my way through, I turn into one of the places I trust enough, and work my way through the casino floor. I wander, though really, I know where I'm going. I take in the smell of cigarette smoke, wondering how many new addicts Vegas creates, because not all bad habits tried just once on a let-loose weekend stay in Vegas. I weave my way through the bleary-eyed folks staring at the slot machines. The excited brokers working the tables with cigars between their lips. I pass the waitresses pasting on fake smiles for the tips.

Maybe I hate this place so much because my only experience is being neck deep in Sin City where people let out the worst of themselves for the weekend. I see all their faults and their wicked fantasies.

Surely things are better outside of this city.

But I got assigned to stay in this area, close to the gate, so here I've stayed.

I weave my way back, further and deeper into the hotel. Soon, there are black walls with neon green lights streaking deeper into the belly of the building. There's a line, dozens of girls dressed like me, here for a good time and wandering eyes. There are plenty of guys with their shirts unbuttoned, their eyes hungry, money in their pockets, ready to buy drinks for pretty girls.

I pay the entry fee, and step into the dark chamber of the club.

It's crowded already, but not as much as I anticipated. It's what you'd expect. There are dozens of people at the bar, getting the drinks that will loosen their mouths, their hips, their legs. There are groups at the tables spread all around the perimeter. Laughing loudly, talking so loud over the music they'll lose their voices by last call or morning. The music pumps loud, loud enough my ears will be ringing when I leave. And the middle of the space is full of people dancing.

I work my way around the club, just watching, observing. I can't help it. After all my years of training, it's what I do. Not that I'm expecting any threats here. The only one I'm worried about is nearly two thousand miles away. It's just not possible, even for him, to travel all that distance in a few hours.

I order a Coke at the bar, settling onto a stool where

I can watch the crowd. A pang of jealousy snips through my stomach. I'm alone. Always alone. I have companions. Over the years they've become family. I love them.

But I don't have friends.

I don't have someone who runs his hands through my hair, puts his hands on my hips.

I wonder how it feels. Because after all this time, I can't remember anymore. And things were much more proper back then.

I'd really, really like to know how it feels.

"Can I buy you a drink?"

My eyes slide over to a guy walking up from the side. He's by himself, but I see a group of three other guys down a ways, watching with bright eyes and leering smiles.

This guy is hot. I won't deny that. Dark, dark hair, the kind of facial hair that everyone is going for these days. His black shirt with white polka-dots hugs a nice form.

But the way his eyes trace me up and down, it's the kind of gaze that makes my skin crawl and all the alarm bells in my body sound off.

"Not tonight," I say, letting my eyes wander back out into the crowd.

"Well, how about room service in the morning?" he asks with a pervy smile growing on his lips as he takes a step closer.

I shoot a dark look at him, daring him with my eyes to come one step closer.

He will regret it.

"Not on your life," I snarl.

"Come on, baby girl, don't be like that," he says. His eyes fix on my chest and he takes a step forward, reaching for my waist.

"Let's hit the floor, babe."

Another body somehow fits between this douchebag and me, and my eyes flick up to meet those of a dangerous and sinfully beautiful man, looking down at me with this expression that just begs to know if I'm okay and need help.

"What took you so long?" I say, both annoyance and relief washing over me as his hand slips to mine, and I let him pull me up from my seat. He leads me away from the slimy guy who I'd really like to make sure doesn't bother any other girls tonight.

I glare darkly over my shoulder at him as this guy leads me toward the middle of the floor.

Mr. Perv just leers after me.

"Sorry," this new guy says, stalling on the other side of the crowd from the bar. "You don't have to say anything, you just looked like you were about to kill that guy if he said another word. Figured you could maybe use an out that didn't involve murder."

A smile pulls on the corners of my mouth.

He could tell, that easily, just from what? Maybe one minute of observation?

"You're not wrong," I say, looking up at him. "He was in serious danger if he didn't back down in point two seconds."

"Just looking out for everybody," he says as a wry smile crooks on one side of his face. "I kind of like this place. Wouldn't want to see it get shut down for a murder investigation."

I smile, taking him in, hoping my evaluation made over five seconds isn't wrong.

He's tall. Taller than six feet, I'm confident. He's toned and muscled in a way that tells me he's exceptionally strict in what he eats and spends a lot of time working out. If I had to guess, I'd say he was around twenty-five, which is lucky, because according to my looks and age when all this madness began, I'm twenty-two and a half.

There's darkness in his green eyes, and I wonder how he can look like that, and be so considerate to save me. His hair is dirty blond and tied back at the nape of his neck. Five days' worth of facial hair hugs one of the most chiseled jaws I've ever seen.

He looks like he can handle himself in just about any situation.

He's gorgeous. Hot. In the bad boy, wrong side of the tracks, kind of way. He even has the low, gravelly voice to match it all.

"You really here by yourself?" he asks, looking around as if a crowd of friends is going to materialize.

"Maybe," I say, giving a non-committal shrug.

He smiles, shaking his head. "You live here, don't you?"

My brows furrow slightly. "How'd you guess?"

He smirks, his eyes rising and running through the crowd again. "One, you are here on your own. Two, you don't seem nervous to be here on your own. Three, you've got that *I will kill you*, tough girl vibe you get after living here for a few years."

I raise an impressed eyebrow at him. "And considering you know all that, I'm going to take a guess that you're also local."

He shrugs, which is answer enough.

"What about you?" I ask, looking around. "You also here alone?"

We step further to the outskirts, leaning against a wall as the crowd grows more dense, the dancers getting more enthusiastic.

"I came here looking for someone," he says, casting his eyes through the crowd again. "But they're not here."

All of my insides darken, and my eyes slide over to him.

"Not a girl," he explains, realizing where my mind has gone. "And not a guy either, just to clarify." He says it with another smirk, and the shadows inside me relax a little. "I've been trying to track my older brother down. He's supposed to be getting a job done, but has a bad habit of sex, drugs, rock and roll, if you know what I mean. But I'm realizing he's trying extra hard not to be found tonight. I'm giving up the search."

There's a lot more there we could talk about. This brother is trouble, and I swear I can already guess the type. This younger brother cares enough, or is desperate enough to get this job done, to go looking on a Friday night on The Strip.

Just this little bit tells me a lot.

But I've already dealt with too much heaviness tonight.

It's not what I came here for.

For just a moment, I feel like I can be human.

"Do you want to dance?" I ask as my heart starts pounding.

His eyes meet mine, and there's this moment of suspension. Like the room has slowed, the music grows quieter, and all of my insides feel like they're floating.

He is exactly what I need tonight.

"Yeah," he answers, that smirk pulling at the corners of his lips again.

I don't suppress my smile as I grab both his hands and pull him back into the heart of the crowd.

The song is medium speed with a good rhythm. I lock my eyes on his, letting my hips sway to the rhythm. He smiles, though it's more hesitant than I would have expected. There's something a little unsure in his hands when they reach my hips.

I smile, tipping my head back, lacing my fingers behind his neck, sinking deeper into the rhythm.

I love to dance. I love music. I love a beat.

Alone in my apartment, I love to turn up my favorite songs and close my eyes and just let my hips move. I've considered it, if I just walked away from the compound, I wouldn't mind getting a job dancing. Letting people watch. Not that I'd ever take my clothes off.

But I truly do love to move.

The song changes, shifting to something deeper, something a little sultrier.

It's a song I love.

A smile crosses my lips and I turn, my back to his front. When I sense his hesitancy, I reach for his hands, bringing them to my hips again, pulling him closer.

"Is this okay?" I ask, turning my head, saying the words so only he can hear them.

"Hell, yeah," he says, leaning closer behind me, his chin brushing my shoulder. I smile again, swaying deeper, relishing every tiny bit of space where we align and connect.

I reach a hand up, hooking it behind his neck, and his chest connects with my back.

My insides ignite, alive and bright.

I love to dance. But I always dance alone.

This guy is a contradiction. His look screams bad boy, his eyes and his words feign confidence. But there's this hesitance when he touches me. I relish in it when he sinks deeper into it by the moment.

"You're a really good dancer," he says, low, right into my ear.

I guide his hand from my hip, wrapping it around my waist, letting our motions become smaller but closer.

"You make a pretty decent partner," I reply, savoring in the feeling of his breath on my neck.

When the song changes to something slower, he turns me under his arm and dips me back, low enough my hair brushes the floor.

I smile and a small laugh comes from my lips. He brings me upright and holds me close. I rest my hand on his chest, my other hand held firmly in his. Slowly, we sway back and forth. I am very aware of his hand on my hip, holding me close and firm.

I haven't had this much fun in…so long…I can't even remember now. I've never been this out of my own head and this into my own body. I've never just let go and been in the moment here and now.

The song changes once more, fast and sexy. I turn, my back against his front again.

He runs his hands up slowly, from my hips, up my

sides, all the way up my arms. A million goose bumps flash over my skin, igniting every inch of me with life. His fingers come up to lace through mine. He slides our hands behind his neck.

He bends down, touching his cheek to mine.

"My name is Jaxon," he says softly into my ear.

I smile a little, because somehow, it's the perfect name for him. Dangerous and simple.

I know he's waiting. I can practically hear him begging for my name.

But I can't.

There's no point.

But I'm not ready for the night to be over either, so I spin, grab his hand, and pull him over to the line that's formed, dancing to an EDM version of The Macarena.

He just rolls with it with a smirk. He blushes just a little, but still, he joins in the ridiculous dance somehow everyone knows.

I laugh and dance, but mostly, I just tell myself to appreciate every single moment of this night, because I probably won't ever repeat it.

And then the music changes again, and it's a slow song. So, I smile, and Jaxon smiles, and I don't hesitate when I loop my arms behind his neck, and I love and hate how natural it feels when he slides his hands around my waist.

"This turned out to be a pretty incredible night,

considering how terrible it started," he says quietly as he looks down at me.

"Yeah," I say, nodding in agreement with a soft smile. "It really did, considering how awful it started."

I could keep looking into his green eyes all night, appreciating his bad boy charm.

But I know the night is growing late.

I feel the clock ticking.

And I know it's going to end.

"Do you think—"

He begins to ask a question I know I can't give a positive answer to when he suddenly stops swaying, his entire body stiffening, his eyes fixing somewhere near the door.

"What?" I ask, turning to see what he's looking at.

There's a man who's just walked in. He's built exactly like Jaxon, just a little shorter. They have the same wild blond hair and the same nose. But there are dark circles under this guy's eyes. There's a fog there that says his mind isn't clear.

"Aaron," a name breathes out over Jaxon's lips.

His brother meets his eyes across the club and he, too, stiffens to stillness. I see Aaron's eyes darken, his shoulders going rigid.

And then he turns and walks back out the door.

"Aaron!" Jaxon yells, taking one automatic step toward the door.

His brother slips out of sight.

Desperate, Jaxon looks back at me, his mouth open.

"I—" he stutters. "I'm sorry. I have to go after him."

"It's okay," I say, feeling something inside of me sinking, but also something like relief that it can end this way and not what I'd already been planning in my head. "Go take care of your brother."

"Can I see you again?" he asks, taking another step toward the door, keeping his eyes fixed on me. He truly looks desperate. And hopeful.

Which breaks my heart.

"I don't think so, Jaxon," I say, feeling my entire body sag in regret.

"Why not?" he asks, his expression faltering.

I shrug as he takes another step away, his brother getting further and further away. "Because we were never meant to meet in the first place."

I see it, the break in his expression, realizing that this is the end. We just had the most incredible night. Such a natural, physical connection.

And now it's just over, and I never even told him my name.

He also doesn't understand my answer.

He just blinks three times, his mouth slightly open, like he wants to say something.

But I can tell. He's a loyal man. Despite his looks, he's a good guy.

He won't force me when I've said no.

"Thank you," he says softly, regret in his voice. "Tonight was amazing."

I offer him a sad smile.

And then he turns and heads for the door.

He turns back though, just before he walks out.

And I hate this. I hate that I've been dealing with loneliness for so long.

I hold his gaze.

And then he's gone, out the door, and I'll never see him again.

Feeling suddenly empty and alone and cold, I look around the club. There are all these people here, all of them happy, having fun. All of them will go back to their regular lives come Monday, but they'll carry these memories to get them through to their next great event.

This? This was a once-in-a-lifetime moment for me. This was something I never do. Something I doubt I'll ever convince myself to do again.

I want to let myself drown in sorrow. The evening started with heartbreak over the loss of Agent Calista. Letting go of this high threatens to drown me further.

But I've survived one hundred percent of my bad days so far. I'll get through this lonely night, as well.

So, I open my eyes, take a deep breath, and I head for the doors.

Jaxon is long gone, of course. Gone to take care of

whatever is going on with his older brother. I step out into the casino, surrounded by strangers. I walk out to the road and join even more of them.

Through the dark, crowded streets, I walk home, alone.

## Chapter Two

I'M SITTING with Renwick at a table in the armory, cleaning guns, when Davorian walks in, a phone pressed to his ear. He waves for the two of us and immediately walks out.

Renwick and I glance at each other, pausing just two seconds before we both spring to our feet, following our boss's quickly retreating form. He hooks into the conference room where Nisha is already waiting, along with Philomena.

Davorian lays his phone on the table and turns it to speaker.

"Say that again, Layla," he says in his booming voice.

"We've been tracking the Kindred the last two days," Layla says on the other end. "He's been moving from Georgia to Kentucky. This morning we tracked him moving up into Colorado and then into Utah. And now it looks like he's turning south. He could be headed for Arizona. But there's just as high of a chance that he'll hook into Nevada."

"Do we know what he's looking for?" Ascelin asks as he sits in a seat next to me.

"I mean, they know we partner in threes," Layla answers. "He was looking for me and Calista before. But once he started moving out of the area… I mean, I have no idea."

I look up, locking eyes with Davorian. I see in his own that he doesn't like this either. The Kindred are one-track minded. Their only reason for organization is to track down and kill us. They're slow at it, but they've been getting the job done.

So, not knowing why he's given up and moved on to another area is bewildering. He was successful in tracking down and killing a darkling. He would know there would be two more in the area.

It's strange.

"We'll be on alert," Davorian says. "I want you back in your station. Stop tailing the Kindred."

"Understood," Layla answers.

Davorian ends the call.

We haven't run into a Kindred since the eighties, and I barely walked away with my life. We keep hoping their group will fall apart, the ultralights know nothing about organization, yet they keep chasing after us, year after year.

"Philomena," Nisha barks, turning to my team member. "I want you patrolling the border. Renwick, I want you out in the city, keeping an eye out."

Each of them simply gives a nod, rising to their feet.

Nisha opens her mouth again to say something else, when a shrill ring pings through the entirety of the compound.

Every single pair of eyes jumps to the bright screen.

Everyone scrambles to their feet.

There are five screens set up next to each other, making one huge, wide map of the entire world. On it, there are thousands of brilliant, glowing white dots.

And now, there is a new one pulsing, glowing brilliant as the sun.

"Now?" Ascelin says, his eyes going wide as he taps on the screen, zooming the satellite image in. We fall into the United States, into the western side.

Farther we fall, zooming in on Nevada. And then further, right in on Las Vegas.

"Here?" I say in disbelief. "Right, right here." I shake my head.

Everyone gathers with wide eyes. Excitement rises in the space.

"Been a long time since a new one glowed that bright," Ascelin observes.

"A really long time," Davorian says. I hear something spark in his voice. Something hopeful. Something urgent.

After the darkness of grief we've all been swimming in the last few days, none of us expected a surge of hope.

"It's been six months since the last one," Philomena says, excitement rising in her own voice. "Maybe… Maybe this will be the one."

"Don't get your hopes up," Renwick says, ever the skeptic as I am. But he, too, leans in closer, looking at the location, blinking brilliant white. "I guess now we know why the Kindred is headed this way."

"Assignments still stand," Nisha says, standing rigid and alert, ever the commander. "Renwick, Philomena, I want you watching. Serena, you'll bring this one in. I want it done fast, before this Kindred can get into the area. I want our hands on him first."

Each of us nods, and instantly we break away to go do our jobs.

I duck into my office and grab my pack. I fasten it first around my waist, and then the second buckle around my thigh. I unzip it, making sure that all the supplies I'll need are in it.

A gun. Bullets. Something to knock a person out. Other essentials.

"I'm sending the coordinates to you," Ascelin says from his post. My phone beeps and I open it up, granted mobile access to the satellite image.

"Shouldn't take more than twenty minutes once I get there," I call out. "I'll see you soon."

Ascelin salutes me and I take off down the passageway. The moment I hit the end of it, I shift, feeling my body rip apart into shadows and black limbs and fangs and claws.

I crawl up the tunnel with no effort at all.

When I reach the top, I shift again and go straight for the motorcycle. I rev it to life, and rip off through the night, headed back toward the city.

They manifest all over the world. It's the reason why we're so spread out. Because once those lights start blinking, we have five to fourteen days before they start to manifest. We have only a little time before the Kindred start looking for them.

We have to get to them first.

The lights of Las Vegas start to glow in the distance. I streak through the evening, flying over the desert. We're nearly an hour out from the city, but I make the journey in forty minutes. The second I roll into town, I aim for my apartment. I screech to a stop in front of my car, dash up the stairs, switch keys, and crash into the driver's seat of my car.

I back up, throwing my phone's screen to the car's

display. It maps out the way to the blinking dot. They're in one of the casinos, right on the Strip.

I take the back roads, knowing it will be ten times faster than fighting my way down the actual Strip. Up several blocks. Then I cut directly over to the parking garage. I roll up to the third level.

I park in the middle, inconspicuous. And then I take my phone out.

The target's location hasn't changed. They're still inside this casino.

A message comes through on my phone, from Renwick, who is apparently on technical assistance duty, even though he's keeping an eye out for the Kindred.

*On the move. You in place?*

*Ready,* I text back.

I log in to the satellite transmission and within five seconds I get zeroed in on my target.

They show up as a brilliant white dot. Just before the ultralights manifest, they start emitting brilliant light, light invisible to the eye. Makes them incredibly easy to track. Easy to tag. Easy to take.

Down, down, down an elevator I watch them descend. I keep my hand on the gearshift, in case I have to switch garage floors. Thankfully there are only four of them here.

It's my lucky day. The elevator slows and then stops

here. I see the figure cut horizontally through the casino, right for the parking garage.

I pull the gun out, resting it in my lap and my eyes slide up to the doors.

I see the door being pushed open.

My entire brain glitches out and I freeze in place.

Jaxon.

Jaxon just walked out of that door.

There's another man with him, younger and more innocent looking than Jaxon. He looks like he's only seventeen or so.

My eyes slide back down to my phone, praying that I'm wrong, that there's been some mistake.

But there isn't. That brilliant light still blinks, exactly where Jaxon and the other man are.

"Crap," I breathe under my breath as I slide down in my seat, trying to stay out of his sight.

I look back down at my phone, trying to get a lock on which one of them I'm after. But they're standing close enough together and the light they're emitting is so bright, I can't differentiate between the two.

I curse under my breath, watching them as they cross the parking garage. They're talking, but in low, hushed tones. I can't hear what they're saying.

I could take them both out. We could test them both. But that would make things so much more complicated and so much messier.

I'm not a fan of messy.

And the second I show my face, Jaxon is going to recognize me.

I need more time to figure this out.

They both walk down just four parking spaces and Jaxon pulls keys from his pocket. They walk up to a wicked looking motorcycle and grab helmets.

The younger one has darker hair than Jaxon. He wears it slicked back like he's trying to look like some baby mobster. But he has Jaxon's same lips, the same shaded eyes.

How many brothers does this guy have?

The younger brother climbs onto the bike behind Jaxon. They back out of the parking spot and I slide further down in my seat to not be seen. I watch as the bike heads toward the exit.

My brain is a constant string of curse words. I know what I need to do. I need to determine which of these two is the one I'm after and bring them back to the compound immediately.

But I know this guy.

I had one of the best nights of my life with him.

And now this?

I don't have time to wait a few seconds and follow behind. With the traffic what it is today, I'll lose them in two seconds. I immediately put the car into drive and head down to ground level.

I would have lost them if I'd waited. I barely catch

sight of them as they turn right onto the same side street I took to get here.

I don't turn on my blinker as I pull onto the road after them.

As the traffic thins, I allow a little bit of distance as we take turn after turn. We head for the less glamorous side of Las Vegas, which, let's face it, is a large portion of Vegas. We roll past all the run-down casinos only the locals go to. Into some of the darker, less well-lit residential streets.

When I see the brake lights of the bike, I slow down as well, stalling in taking this last turn.

I watch as Jaxon parks on the side of the road. He lowers the kickstand, and they both climb off.

I pull around the corner, parking five houses down, on the opposite side of the street.

Jaxon walks in front, and I wonder at the strange set of his shoulders, the thinness of his lips.

He looks like he doesn't want to be here.

He looks like he already regrets whatever is about to happen.

They walk right up to the door and Jaxon knocks, muttering something to the younger one.

I roll my windows down, letting in the hot air, so I can hear.

"You don't have to do anything," Jaxon says. "If it comes to breaking bones, I don't want you getting your hands dirty."

"This is getting really old, Jaxon," the younger boy says. "If Mom says it's time, it's time. Nothing you can do about it."

"You're sixteen years old," Jaxon says. "You're supposed to be in school. Going to homecoming with some girl. Wouldn't you rather be doing that?"

"Doesn't matter," the younger boy says. But he doesn't get to say anything else, because the door to the house opens.

Jaxon immediately grabs the guy who answers by the front of his shirt, walking him inside three steps, before slamming him against a wall.

My eyes widen, and I blink five times.

I never, ever would have called this.

I don't catch all the words, but basically Jaxon has come to collect on a gambling debt. The guy getting attacked hasn't been answering their calls. "Mom" says it's time to pay up. And they take payment in the form of cash or fingers and toes.

I look back down at my phone when fists start getting thrown. There's the satellite image, glowing brilliant and bright. There's no mistaking it. One of those two is an ultralight.

But it doesn't make any bit of sense.

Ultralights are good people. At least they start out that way. It's a basic qualification. They're good and loyal people that can be trusted to defend this verse. They manifest literal *light*.

But I look up at the two figures still barely visible from the door and see them swing and bash.

I know these types. They're all over Vegas. If you can't pay in cash, they'll take a pound of flesh, maybe more, in interest.

They're not the kind of people you'd trust the safekeeping of your planet with.

The brawl rolls out of my sight, and through the shades of a window, I see the man flee, trying to get away. But he's caught. There's more hitting. There's a yell.

Jaxon is a beast. He looks like he could be a professional MMA fighter. With fists and kicks, he looks like he could kill this guy.

I swallow, at once horrified and mesmerized by the way he moves.

If they don't calm this party down, someone is going to call the cops any second.

I duck further down in my seat.

This could be harder than I'd thought.

Somehow, I have to figure out which of these two boys is the ultralight. Somehow, I have to get whichever is my guy back to the compound.

Unfortunately, they both know how to handle themselves.

I look back down at the phone again, making sure the light is still glowing. It is.

My heart jumps into my throat with the sharp crack of a gunshot. My eyes flick back to the house.

The night is still. It's quiet.

And then three seconds later, I see Jaxon backing up out of the house, dragging the younger boy, who looks exceptionally limp.

As Jaxon drags him down the sidewalk, I see a trail of blood smear behind the boy.

All of my insides go cold. There's something in me that screams out in horror. I fight the instinct to run out to Jaxon and help.

But I can't. I have to stay here, hidden.

It's no small feat, loading a body onto a motorcycle. I've never had to do it, but the logic just isn't there.

Yet somehow Jaxon does it. He secures the younger boy, who doesn't move. And just as a little old lady on the other side of the street steps out onto her porch, he pulls away from the curb.

I curse again under my breath and my eyes snap to my phone.

That'd be just our luck. To find another ultralight, just for him to get killed before he even manifests.

But a trickle of calm slips down the back of my neck when I look at my screen, and still see a glowing white light, moving quickly away from my location.

He's the one. Jaxon is the ultralight I'm after.

## Chapter Three

"Have you got them?" Renwick's voice cuts through the speaker system of my car.

"Things got a little complicated," I answer, my eyes focused on the road ahead of me. Through the fading light, I watch as Jaxon drives the motorcycle. "I'm still working on it."

"This is a new record for you, and not in a good way," Renwick says through clenched teeth. "Pretty sure you've never taken more than ten minutes once you've gotten a target within sight."

"Shut your trap, Ren," I growl. My mood is turning more sour by the moment, because he's right. This is totally messing up my numbers. "Turns out this guy is a shylock and there were guns involved, and now he's dragging a body around the city."

"For real?" my fellow agent asks in surprise.

"Stranger than fiction," I say, letting out a hard breath through my nose. And I haven't even mentioned the night we had together.

"You owe me a story later," he says. He knows I need to get back to this mission. "Good luck out there."

"Thanks," I quip before ending the call.

It's quiet on this side of the city. Jaxon drives deeper into the residential part of town. The houses grow bigger here, nicer. There's a gate that we drive through, though it isn't closed and there's no guard. I guess it's purely for looks and an attempt at status.

Jaxon loops through the neighborhood and doesn't hesitate when he pulls into the driveway of a very nice home.

I park two doors down, grateful that Jaxon is distracted by his injured brother and has no idea he's being tailed. Through the dark, I watch.

Jaxon heaves the younger boy over his shoulders in a fireman's carry, muttering to the boy to hang in there, to stay awake.

It kind of breaks my heart. Jaxon thinks his brother is still alive.

He stumbles his way to the front door and then kicks at it, calling out for a Dr. Jeshem.

Six seconds later, a man who looks to be in his sixties opens the door, eyes wide behind his thick glasses. With a start, he steps aside, letting Jaxon in.

I look around, making sure that no one is watching. It's quiet. This is the kind of neighborhood that has a lot of families, so on this Sunday night, most people will be heading to bed right now.

No one is looking out their windows.

I slip out of my car, zipping my keys into my coat pocket.

I cut across yards, slipping behind bushes, and then hop the fence into the backyard of the good doctor. It's a nice place, with a pool and actual grass. But my eyes are searching the back of the house, trying to see where they went.

I watch as a trail of lights flick on, leading up the second story.

I walk to the back of the house, shifting mid reach, letting my legs jut out, gripping even the tiniest of holds. In dark shadows, I scale the side of the house, lifting and pulling my shifting form onto a roof, watching with keen eyes as the lights trail to one end, just to the side of the garage.

I move over to that side of the house, utterly silent. As soon as I reach a semi-flat surface, I suck in the shadows, shifting back into my human form.

Quietly, I slide under the window, looking through.

It's an office, but more like a doctor's office. There's a table in the middle of it and cupboards that line the wall. The doctor works in a flurry on the boy, now laid on the table.

He's gone.

I know that.

I know that doctor knows that.

But he's still got to try, even if it's only for Jaxon's sake.

Jaxon stands in the corner, his hands fisted into his blond hair, his eyes bloodshot with emotion, his expression full of agony.

"I told Mom he was too young to be going out," Jaxon hisses between his teeth. "I told her he wasn't ready."

The doctor doesn't say anything in response, only packs more and more gauze into the wound, which isn't bleeding like it should if his heart were still beating.

The doctor starts chest compressions, but they're halfhearted.

"This is the life you live, Jaxon," the doctor grinds out as he presses on the boy's chest, over and over. "This is the world you were born into."

I see utter agony on Jaxon's face, anger and frustration and regret.

Maybe I made some hasty assumptions about him. I sometimes forget that we don't always get to choose our circumstances.

The doctor slows, fewer and fewer chest compressions.

And then he stops.

He just looks down at the young boy.

I look back at Jaxon.

I see it in his eyes the moment he realizes. I think I see something break. I see the grief flash through him in a second.

And then I see the need for revenge.

I watch as his hands curl into fists.

"I'll send someone for him," Jaxon says, his voice a low growl, dangerous and barely audible.

"Jaxon, wait," the doctor calls out as Jaxon steps out the door, back into the hall. I can't see them, but I can still hear them. "You know how things go when you take the route of revenge. Look at your uncle. Look what it did to your mother. You say you want out, but this? This is how you stay locked in, for life."

I hear shoes crossing tile and then suddenly stop, as if Jaxon stopped at the door, glaring back at the doctor.

"And who would I be if I let my brother's killer keep wandering the streets of my city?"

Something inside me chills. My heart races.

I don't want to sympathize with an ultralight.

"Then it will probably be you on my table next," the doctor says quietly.

I hear a door open, footsteps, and then the door slamming closed.

With a single step, I shift, the black spindles of legs shooting out of me, carrying me silently and confidently across the tile roof. Down the side of the house I climb, and around to the front.

With darkling eyes, I watch Jaxon climb back on his motorcycle, back out of the driveway, and pull down the road.

The second he turns a corner, I scramble across the street, shifting as I reach for the handle of my car. I shove the keys in the ignition and flip around, aiming to catch up with Jaxon.

I shouldn't let this drag on. He's distracted. He should be easy to grab right now. I could take him, I could knock him out, and in an hour, we would know if he's the one we're looking for or not.

But something is holding me back. Maybe it's my own moral compass, saying it's not okay to abduct a man who's just watched his brother get shot. Maybe it's my own curiosity, dying to know who this man actually is, because he's nothing like the rest of them.

I'm not doing my job, and that's a first.

I know where we're headed when he aims back toward the nastier part of town. But once more he surprises me.

He slows as he rolls down the street we were on previously. His eyes are fixed on that house with the bloodstain that is already gone, a water sprayed puddle already evaporating.

I wonder what's going through his head. If he's

remembering the doctors' words. I don't actually know him, so I can't even begin to guess.

But in the end, after a slow roll of contemplation, he moves on. He reaches the end of the street and turns left.

I trail behind, rolling slow and lagging, having a feeling I know where he's going next.

We end up back at the casino. He parks on the third level of the garage again, and I park far enough away he won't see me.

I watch as he gets off his bike, straps his helmet to it, and walks in through that door.

I can only push it so far and not be caught. I'm nearly invisible by supernatural nature. But I wait here for sixty seconds.

I pull out my phone once again, pulling up the satellite imagery. I watch him walk back to the elevator, glowing like a supernova. He rises and I count how many seconds.

Three, four, five. Eleven, twelve.

He rises up to the fifteenth floor.

He walks halfway down the hall, and steps into a space that faces The Strip.

I step out of my car. I walk through the doors.

The scent of smoke and alcohol hits me with force. In this day and age, smoking is a dying habit, but people have a tendency to let the bad choices fly here in Vegas. It's all a good time, and everything stays here, right?

Welcome to a lifetime addiction and say goodbye to your health and money.

I press the button to the elevator, looking around as I wait.

No one seems out of the ordinary. It's just the usual scene. People playing games, staring at the slot machines. Waitresses bustle around, bringing drinks, smiling sweetly.

The doors open and I step inside with two others. I press the button for the fifteenth floor, and up we go.

I think I'm expecting something more dramatic when the elevator doors slide open. Maybe a hall full of mobsters and criminals. Maybe to be met with Jaxon pointing a gun in my face.

But it's just a hallway full of doors.

I step out and aim down the hall, toward where I'm guessing Jaxon went.

I'm just about to turn a corner, when voices cut through the space.

"It's going to be every single one of us, one by one."

I've only heard him speak a few times, but I take good notes when I'm working. I know it's Jaxon.

"You're acting like this is the norm," another voice says. "In the twenty years our family has been in this business, AJ's the first to die. You should have been more careful with him."

There's a beat of silence and I glance around the corner.

Jaxon stands down the hall, talking to another man. The man is slightly taller than Jaxon, but his hair is the exact same shade of blond, though this one sports a full-on beard, which trickles down to his chest. He looks like a complete Viking.

"I told everyone he wasn't ready, that he was too young," Jaxon says, his eyes cold and hard. "He wasn't ready. He panicked in there and look what happened."

"I'm going to miss him too," the other man says. "But life moves on. Don't lose your balls over this."

The man turns, heading toward a door.

"Moves on," Jaxon calls after him, horror and disgust in his voice. "Our brother has been dead less than an hour and you're telling me to move on?"

The other man looks over his shoulder with a glare. I do see pain in his eyes. But also acceptance.

He pushes the door open and steps inside.

Jaxon stands there, alone in the hall. The set of his shoulders is tense, tight. I can hear his hard breaths, all the way down here at the end of the hall.

You start to recognize people who are on the verge of cracking.

You recognize when people are about to lose it.

Jaxon is two breaths from that.

He steps forward, pushing the door open.

And just then, I hear the elevator doors ding open. Looking back, I see another man pushing what certainly looks to be a coffin out of the elevator.

I scramble forward, slipping further down the hall, turning a corner, just before the man steps into the hall.

I slip into shadows, drifting around the corner, keeping a visual.

The hard-looking man pushes the cart down the hall, and I'm more and more certain that it is indeed a coffin.

What kind of people have access to a coffin and can load up a body, in less than an hour?

They both disappear into the same room.

*What's taking so long?*

My phone vibrates with the text message, almost immediately popping up with another.

*I'm sending back up.*

*No,* I respond back. *I've got this under control. Just…a weird situation.*

*Nisha says you've got an hour, and then she's sending in Philomena to help.*

*I'VE GOT THIS,* I respond, hoping he gets my emphasis and how serious I am. *I've never failed on bringing in a target before, have I? Have a little faith.*

Three little dots stare at me for a minute before his response comes back.

*Two hours. That's the best I can do.*

*Fine,* I reply. *Two hours. No one steps in a second before that.*

*Fine,* Renwick's reply comes back, and I can just hear his mocking, snappy tone.

I know I'll figure it out, but really, I'm not entirely sure how I'm going to deal with this.

I'm blind and deaf right now. I can't see into that room, and I can't hear anything behind that door.

So, I walk to the end of the hall. I knock on a door to be sure the room is empty, and I sit on the floor like I've been locked out of the room. The door Jaxon disappeared behind is just barely in my line of sight.

I pull my phone out and check the satellite once more.

Jaxon is inside. I know this. But I don't get a reading on the other people in the room. Our scanners only detect ultralights, and no one else inside is one of those.

How many family members does this guy have? So far, I know of AJ, who is now dead. The drugged-out older brother. The one who looks like a viking. I'm guessing the guy pushing the cart with the coffin is also family. They look similar enough.

I know I heard other voices in the room, too.

Twenty minutes later, I hear the door opening again and I roll out of sight, just as a woman steps out into the hall.

Silent and careful, I creep around the corner to look.

A woman wearing black steps out, followed by another woman, followed by the two older brothers I saw.

One, two, three, four, five, and then Jaxon steps out. Followed by the coffin being pushed by a new guy, and then an older woman.

All family?

I don't know.

But I let them disappear down the elevators.

How are they not worried about freaking people out by pushing a coffin around a casino on the Strip?

I keep an eye on my phone, watching as Jaxon descends to the third level parking floor, and then I head for the elevator myself. Down and down, and he pulls away when I hit the parking garage.

I monitor him as I climb into my car, and I follow behind several blocks.

Jaxon might be distracted, might not notice me, but his other family members might.

I don't know a lot about funerals on this side, but this doesn't seem right. This doesn't feel official in any way. I feel like more people should be involved. I'm pretty sure normal people do memorials and services. I'm pretty sure a mortician is supposed to be involved.

But there was no time for any of that. There will be no police investigation. Not with these kinds of people. AJ got packed up and put away in a matter of minutes and here we already are at a cemetery, in the middle of the night.

I can see a hole dug already, an undertaker standing there, waiting like he, too, can't wait to get this over with.

I guess this is what a criminal's funeral looks like.

None of this makes sense.

I don't understand how Jaxon can be an ultralight if he's living a life like this.

The family parks near the burial site and I watch as four strong men climb out and unload the casket. Two young women join side by side with a stony-faced woman who looks a little bit like them all.

Silently, they head for the hole.

I watch from my car, parked far enough away that I'm just anyone in the world.

I'm almost positive they're all family. They have similar looks. But they certainly don't look close, like I'd expect. They stand far apart from each other for the most part. There's this air of tension about them all. Like no one knows who to cast the blame on.

Considering how Jaxon stands entirely on his own, I'd guess they blame him the most.

I decide then. I'll cause a distraction when they leave the cemetery. Somehow, I'll get Jaxon on his own, shouldn't be too hard. And I'll take him then.

I was patient and courteous enough to wait this long.

I don't have time to let him go home and grieve tonight.

My phone goes off again and I hiss in annoyance at Renwick's impatience.

But my blood runs cold as I read the message.

*The Kindred is here. Streaking around Vegas. Keep your eyes peeled.*

Adrenaline instantly surges in my blood. My eyes dilate, letting in more light, enhancing my vision. My insides halfway shift, increasing my hearing. All the tiny hairs on my arms and the back of my neck stand on end.

I'm monster on the inside, human, for now, on the outside.

*I'll lay low,* I text back to Ren. *Probably be best to leave the target alone for now. But I'll keep an eye on him. Let me know if you hear anything else definitive.*

It takes him a long minute to respond. He knows what all of this means. I can't go back to the compound, I can't risk leading the Kindred to them. Neither can he or Philomena.

We're out here with this Kindred on our own.

*Let us know if you need back up,* Ren responds.

*Will do.*

I swear under my breath, setting my phone aside with the shake of my head.

As if this night wasn't off kilter enough.

My eyes rise back up to the funeral.

Only they're all gone. Frantically, I search through the cemetery, and find the crew heading back to their cars, the event already done and over.

But I count.

One, two, three, four, five, six…

The passenger door of my car is yanked open, a body slips in, and I'm looking down the shiny barrel of a handgun.

My eyes shift up to meet Jaxon's green eyes.

"Who the hell are you really?" he growls. His gaze is cold as steel, and his hand does not shake. "And why have you been following me?"

My eyes shift back over to his family, all in vehicles now, every one of them pulling away, leaving just Jaxon and I here.

"You a cop?" he asks, his voice low and dangerous.

"I'm not a cop," I say, slowly holding my hands up.

"Then why are you following me?" he demands, sliding the gun through the air, inching closer to my face.

"Because I need you," I say, stalling.

Something across the cemetery catches my eye. A movement in the dark.

"What is that supposed to mean?" Jaxon demands.

A figure steps out from behind a large tombstone. He stands there, clothed from head to toe in all white.

His glowing white eyes are fixed on me.

I curse, feeling time slow down, as the Kindred steps forward, his fists igniting and glowing a white so brilliant, it's almost blue.

"Put on your seatbelt," I say, lowering my hand to the gear shift.

"Don't move until you answer my questions!" Jaxon bellows at me, jabbing the gun harder at me.

The Kindred sprints across the cemetery, his feet, his legs, his entire body igniting into brilliant, blinding light. I partway shift, half a dozen spindly legs springing from my body, shadows slithering out to fill the car.

One of my legs flicks out, yanking the gun from Jaxon's grip, another shoves him back against his seat.

He gives a terrified yell, curse words slipping from his lips.

I throw the car into reverse, my wheels screaming against the pavement as we're thrown backwards.

"I said put on your seatbelt!" I yell, keeping my eyes fixed on the Kindred who streaks like a missile over the gravestones.

I throw the car into gear and we bullet forward.

"What the hell?" Jaxon screams, scrambling to get away from my spindles and shadows. His face is ghostly white, his eyes wide and terrified.

I hold him pinned against his seat, checking the rear-view mirror as we rip down the quiet street.

The Kindred darts out into the road, slipping and sliding as he attempts to change direction.

I swear again and lay harder on the gas.

"What the hell are you?" Jaxon screams, fighting against my grip, sinking into utter terror as he witnesses half of my monster form.

If only he saw the full shift.

He'd probably be passed out already.

"You're about to learn all about what I am and what you are," I say, leaning hard as I rip around a corner, aiming for the edge of the city, thankful that the cemetery was already toward the outskirts.

My eyes slide back to the rearview mirror and widen in horror as I watch the Kindred turn sonic white, and leap through the air.

"Hold on!" I bellow, laying harder on the gas, knowing it won't be enough.

I shift fully as the impact happens. I let go of every shred of control, letting my full being explode into this world. I grow, I lengthen. I feel strong, invincible. My shadows dart out, filling every space of the vehicle.

I engulf Jaxon as the Keeper collides with the car. As it explodes into a million shards of metal and rubber and fabric.

Jaxon and I roll together. I cradle him into my body with my legs. We roll down the street, shrapnel embedding itself into my back, my skull, my legs.

But as we come to a slow, I get to my feet, letting out an unearthly shriek as I turn to the Kindred.

Jaxon lies on the ground, his head bleeding, blinking in disbelief at the scene before him.

A black, demon monster, and a floating, glowing angel of death.

"He'll kill you if he catches you," I say. In this form, my voice comes out deep and in a wave of shivers and sounds. "Hide."

It's a lie.

But I need him.

With shaking arms, he crawls over to another car, climbing underneath it.

The Kindred darts forward, a nearly invisible streak of light.

I dart four legs out at him, gripping him by the throat and throwing him against a telephone pole with everything I have. I don't wait one second before I skitter forward, pinning his arms and legs down, breathing in the darkness, sucking the light out of him.

We're mortal enemies. By nature, we need to kill each other, because neither of us should exist to the other.

I suck his light, even though it burns every bit of me inside.

But with a pulse of light, he blasts me backward and I go flying through the air, legs and shadows grappling through the midnight dark, desperate for purchase.

"You've taken enough of us," the Kindred says, his voice sonic and crystal. "Your end is coming. It is time for the darklings to accept it."

"Not on your life," I hiss, claws scraping against the pavement.

I run. I bound. I leap through the air, jaw extending wide, fangs exposed.

He doesn't react fast enough. I sink my teeth into his neck, yanking as we roll together.

The Kindred gives a deafening howl as we flip over. But he reaches forward, digging his glowing hands into my slick flesh, light burning right through my skin.

I release his neck, legs flying and claws snapping at him, prying his fingers out of my flesh.

"The end of the darklings is imminent," the Kindred says as he climbs to his feet, wiping a hand over his bleeding neck. "Why fight it?"

"Because I have my own home to get back to," I growl back.

He glows brighter.

I crouch, shifting bigger. Sprouting a few more legs. Growing more teeth.

And I pounce.

I wrap my entire body around his, squeezing and compressing tighter and tighter. My shadows slip into his nostrils, searching for their way into his lungs.

Brighter and brighter, hotter and hotter.

A wicked sound erupts from my maw as the pain grows and grows as his light turns blinding.

With every last ounce of strength I have, I flex. I grip him by his stupid white shirt. I wind.

And I throw him with everything I have.

He launches through the air, flying across the park.

He lands on the roof of the pavilion. His head lolls to the side and his arm flings out limply.

He's not dead.

I know he's not dead.

But it's got to be enough.

I skitter back down the road. Jaxon gives a terrified yell and scream as I reach beneath the car, pulling him out with my claws.

Up and down the street I look. And I take off for the sideroad with houses.

"Let me go!" Jaxon yells, fighting and clawing to get out of my grip. I hold him by the front of his shirt, lifting him three feet off the ground. "Just let me go!"

We turn down a road and I aim for an old Toyota parked at the curb. I let my shadows slip through the door, unlocking it. I yank the door open with my claws and throw Jaxon into the passenger seat.

I shift instantly as I slip into the driver's seat and immediately set to hotwiring the car.

"Don't run," I growl at him, glaring darkly. "I will catch you."

He grabs the door, and I let one single leg form, pinning him back against his seat.

"Don't run," I hiss again, just as the wires catch and the car starts. Not waiting two seconds, I throw the car into gear and peel out down the road.

I turn right down the road, my eyes flicking across the park.

The Kindred still lies on the roof of the pavilion, though I see he's still breathing.

Such a shame.

"You have no idea who you're messing with," Jaxon growls, switching tactics. "My family isn't one you want to be messing with. They will find you, and they will make you regret taking me."

"You think I'd be afraid of them?" I ask darkly, looking over at him.

He blanches white, and looks away, very deliberately not looking down at the black leg holding him pinned to his seat.

"I'm not going to kill you," I say, fixing my eyes on the road ahead of me. The onramp looms ahead. "The plan was to only take you in for an hour or so, but that guy back there created a huge complication."

Speaking of. I search my pockets, before my stomach sinks.

My phone was sitting in the cupholder of my car.

It's been obliterated.

"Where are we going?" Jaxon asks, his voice hoarse

and low, like he's accepting that this is happening and he's not getting out.

"Away," I answer simply, because I don't really know. "We need to get out of town for a couple of days. I need to call someone. Warn the others."

"Others like you?" he asks, another spike of fear in his voice.

"Others like me," I confirm. My eyes flick to the rearview mirror. I don't see any signs of the Kindred following us. But that doesn't mean I'll let my guard down. "Look, I'll explain everything very soon. But right now, I need to think."

And maybe it's just because he's too shocked to know what to say, but Jaxon shuts up, looks out the window, and accepts his fate.

If only he knew what was coming.

## Chapter Four

I WASN'T EVEN THINKING about a direction. I hit the freeway and just drove. I was aware that I was bleeding. Jaxon was bleeding. But I knew what might happen if that Kindred caught up to us. So, I just kept on driving.

I ended up going northeast. Through the desert we drove in silence. The heat crept higher and higher and there was no AC in this car. It got more and more miserable.

When I saw a sign for a hotel somewhere in the strip of freeway between Nevada and Utah, I pulled off the freeway. It was still the middle of nowhere. There were maybe fifty houses. To our luck, there was a twenty-four-hour Dollar General first thing off the ramp.

"Wipe your face off," I say as we park in the middle

of the tiny parking lot. "And please tell me you have a wallet on you."

"What, you're going for kidnapping and robbery?" he asks snidely.

I just glare at him. "We need some supplies so we don't bleed to death."

"What, no hospitals?" he taunts, though he grabs a sweatshirt that was sitting in the backseat of our stolen vehicle and starts wiping at the blood on his face.

"You think you can explain what just happened?" I quip, wiping my own blood away.

It doesn't work great.

He just glares at me and keeps cleaning himself off.

We still look like we've been to hell and back, but it'll have to do.

Jaxon must be convinced he can't outrun me, because he doesn't try to get away when we step out of the car. He doesn't alert the cashier who scrolls through her phone without even looking up at us.

I grab medical supplies. Everything they have. Which isn't as much as I'd like it to be. Gauze. Disinfectant. A simple sewing kit. I get some anti-inflammatory pain killers. And Jaxon pays in cash.

Maybe criminals don't have credit cards. He would have been smart to use one, some kind of beacon for when his family realizes he's gone.

Convenient for me.

The barely post-high school girl looks at us suspiciously as she rings us up, but she doesn't say a single word beside the total.

I grab the bag and Jaxon's arm and go back out to the car. I get it running again and drive two blocks down the road before pulling into the parking lot of a seedy motel.

Two minutes later, we walk out of the lobby with two room keys. With nothing more than our Dollar General bag, we walk up to the second story and down to room 211.

The room smells slightly of smoke and everything is dated by about fifteen years, but it looks clean enough to not give me an STD.

All the pain and exhaustion I've been ignoring in the past forty-five minutes hits me the second I walk in the door.

I walk straight to the mirror, flipping on the flickering florescent light.

It's worse than I thought.

Bruises are blooming along the left side of my face. There's a nice cut running down my right cheek.

I peel my t-shirt off, and immediately my eyes go to the dark black marks, the perfect shape of fingers dug into my skin.

"Holy…"

In the mirror, my gaze shifts over my shoulder to Jaxon. He stares at my bruised and injured body, particularly those finger marks.

"Pretty sure you look worse," I say, noting the cut above his eye that's bleeding again.

He takes several steps forward, coming into the light. He grabs a towel from the rack, pressing it to the cut. But he never takes his eyes off me.

"I swear," I say. "I'm not going to kill you. I'm not going to eat you either. I just need something from you, and then you'll be free to go."

"Are you stalking me?" Jaxon asks. Even though we're standing side by side, he looks at me in the mirror. "Because that night…"

"I didn't know that night," I said, looking sharply up at him in the mirror. "Us meeting that night was purely coincidence. There was nothing ulterior going on that night, I swear."

He's quiet for a second, and as I look into his eyes in the mirror, I realize how desperately I want him to believe me.

I shouldn't want that.

"You're hurt," he says simply.

I look back at my own reflection. I look like crap. "I've been through worse. I'll survive. You need stitches though."

He leans forward, looking at the cut closer in the mirror. The gash going down his face, from his temple, down the side of his eye, down to his cheek bone, is starting to bleed badly again.

I grab the sewing kit.

"You done this before?" he asks, eyeing me warily.

I set the kit on the countertop and grab his arms, positioning him under the light. I take a towel, get it wet, and set to cleaning the wound.

"More than a couple of times," I say, not meeting his eyes as I work.

"You military?" he asks. I can feel his eyes fixed on me.

"No," I answer simply.

"Military experiment?" he asks, and his tone is dead serious. I guess I can't blame him for that.

"No," I say, my tone getting a little sharper as I set the towel down and thread a needle.

"Alien," he says simply, like it's the last possible explanation.

"I'm not an alien," I say, my tone bordering on offended. "You're never, ever going to guess what I am. So how about you just stop?"

"Then how about you just explain it?" Jaxon says with a growl. He hisses as I dig the needle through his flesh for the first stitch. "Because I thought you were just a really amazing woman I had a really amazing night with. But it turns out you're something a whole lot more interesting."

His choice of words snaps my eyes to his.

He's looking at me with this expression that doesn't fit any of my expectations considering everything that's happened in the last few hours.

He's scared. I can tell that.

But he's not calling me a monster. He's not trying to run away. He's not looking for a way to kill me.

"Just let me finish these stitches first, and then take a shower, okay?" I say, all the fight seeping out of me.

I'm exhausted. And in pain. And I don't know what to do right now.

"Fine," he says gruffly.

He winces as I stitch up the two-inch-long cut. He's lucky he still has his eye. "It's going to scar," I say as I snip the thread. "But at least it's done bleeding."

Jaxon turns and looks in the mirror at my handiwork. It must not be too bad. He doesn't say anything.

I turn and walk into the bathroom, shutting the door behind me.

All the tiny cuts on my body sting as I shower. I seldom feel them in my darkling form. It's as if I exist in a state of adrenaline, impervious to injury. But the second I'm human again, it all hits.

I once stayed a darkling for an entire month, out in the desert. It was the last time I'd run into a Kindred. I'd barely walked away with my life, and I knew that the second I shifted back into human form, all of the pain was going to hit with crippling force.

I knew this was a seedy place. Only fifteen minutes into the shower, the water starts turning lukewarm. At least I got my hair washed.

I shut the water off and wrap a towel around myself.

I stare down at my dirty and bloody clothes on the floor.

The very last thing I want to do is put them on. So I only pull on my underwear and my bra.

I step out into the room, and suddenly realize just how much I trusted Jaxon. Which I never do. I shouldn't have dared to leave him alone. He should have run. He should be at some payphone, calling the government, alerting them that some spider-shadow monster is here, capable of terrible, inhuman things.

But he sits there on the bed, his forearms braced on his knees.

Those pretty green eyes rise to meet mine the second I step out. He takes me in, dressed in nothing but my underthings. But he doesn't say a word, and he doesn't move a muscle.

I cross the room and crawl up onto the other bed. I flop onto it, laying on my back. I stare up at the ceiling, contemplating how to start for several long moments.

This has never been my job. I capture them. I bring them to the gate. We test them. And then we knock them out, putting them back where we found them, and let them manifest and figure things out on their own.

That's not going to work here.

He's seen too much. Knows who I am. Has this tie to me now that I can't deny.

And we live within a quarter mile of each other.

"I'm not an alien," I begin. "I'm not genetically engineered. I'm not something created in a lab." I blink, staring up at the ceiling. My heart is beating faster. I don't want to mess this up. "But I'm not exactly from this world either."

"You said you're not an alien," he says, his voice even, calm.

"You know that whole parallel universes theory?" I ask. I let my mind drift back through the gate, to the other side.

"I guess," Jaxon says. "Something about how there are endless universes out there, with endless versions of us, making every infinite choice possible."

"It's kind of like that," I say, feeling something scrunch in my stomach. Something tightens my throat. "Except there are just two versions."

I close my eyes, squeezing them tight.

"Where you were born, this side, is the Light-Verse," I say, and that something in my stomach twists. "And the side where I was born, where my kind are from, is the DarkVerse."

He doesn't say anything now. I should look over at him, read his expression, but I'm just too tired.

"Each side has these…protectors, that form," I

continue. "I think it's where the LightVerse got the idea for angels."

Just saying the word makes my jaw clench, makes my fingers roll into fists.

I know what angels are supposed to be like. I've heard stories, seen movies about them.

"They're called ultralights," I say, fighting my turning stomach. "What you saw back there, the glowing guy? That's what he was."

"You sound insane right now," Jaxon says. His tone is hard, but I can hear it there as well: he's seen what he's seen.

"The DarkVerse and the LightVerse are opposites of each other in most ways," I say, ignoring him. "I'm the DarkVerse's version of an ultralight. A protector there. A darkling."

The word hangs in the air, thick and heavy and real.

He could deny it, question it, laugh at it. But he saw it. With his own eyes, he saw the reality of what I am.

"There's a gate from this verse to my own," I say, knowing I'm barely scratching the surface. But it's just been too much, been too tiring to go through every detail right now. "A long time ago, a bunch of my kind were on this side, fighting the ultralights. But the gate closed, and we were trapped here."

Jaxon makes this huffing laugh sound. I can only

imagine what's going through his head. I'm telling him all these crazy sounding things. I'm expecting him to believe them.

"How long ago was that supposed to be?" he asks. His tone is slightly mocking. "A year or so ago?"

A little laugh slides over my own lips and my eyes close. "More like 158 years, as of last month."

My eyes slide over to Jaxon with this answer.

He looks at me with narrowed eyes. "What?"

I let my gaze shift back to the ceiling. Sleep pulls heavy on my brain. I'm tired. I can't focus right now.

"I swear, I didn't know who you were when we met at the dance club," I say, sinking back into that perfect night. "I was just looking to destress. Have some fun. I didn't think we'd ever see each other again."

"How did you find out where I live?" Jaxon asks.

I shake my head. "I didn't. It's my job to track down ultralights before they manifest. They're born randomly, but they don't show up until they're young adults. Always around your age, somewhere in the early twenties. We have a way to track when new ones are about to wake up. We've been looking for a special one ever since we got stuck here. So, the darklings have spread throughout the world so we can find them. It only happens a few times a year. But today the system went off. Started glowing brighter than we've seen in a long time."

I turn my head, looking over at Jaxon.

He just looks at me, his eyes narrowed.

He has no idea what's coming.

"It was you, Jaxon," I explain. "You're what set off our system. That's why I showed up at your casino and started following you."

His jaw tenses, and I can tell there are a thousand thoughts running through his mind, a thousand miles an hour. I'm not exactly explaining it well.

"You're an ultralight," I say, dropping the truth on him.

He doesn't say anything. He just stares at me with that hard look. But I can see him thinking it all over.

"I'm exhausted," I say, looking back up at the ceiling. "You need sleep. I...I can explain everything better in the morning."

I feel Jaxon's eyes on me, feel his intense stare. But he doesn't say anything more than, "Okay."

I roll onto my side, away from him, and pull the blankets up and over me, chilled by the air conditioning.

I listen to him through the dark. Hear him pull down the covers, hear him slip inside.

And then it's silent. It's dark.

And I know that come morning, everything is going to get even more complicated.

# Chapter Five

It's the pain that wakes me.

My entire back aches. The burn marks in my side are flaring up again. I wince as I roll over in bed, letting out a curse.

I open my eyes as I roll, and scramble back across the bed when I find myself face to face with Jaxon.

"What are you doing?" I demand as I push my hair out of my face. "Trying to scare me to death?"

"You're the one who turns into a monster," he says calmly. He's sitting on the edge of his bed, his forearms braced against his knees. He's staring at me intensely, as if he's searching for the answer to something.

"Darkling, asshole," I growl. "No one but us gets to call us monsters. It's offensive."

He gives a tiny smirk and a huff of a laugh. But his expression quickly sobers, and I see a shift in his eyes.

"Your face already looks better. Which, isn't possible that fast."

"Yeah, I heal a little faster than your average person," I say as my heartbeat begins to calm just a little bit.

I see him swallow once. He's pale.

"I need you to do it again," he says, his eyes never once leaving mine. "I need to be sure I didn't dream it up last night."

I'm about to ask him *what* he wants me to do again, but I already know the answer.

He wants proof. He wants another visual.

"Don't run," I say again. Because I do not want to chase after him.

"I won't," he promises, and in that moment, I realize that he truly is brave. He knows what he's about to see, but he's going to face it.

I nod once, preparing myself. Shifting into my darkling form is natural to me. But doing it in front of someone else? That can get you killed.

Jaxon never once takes his eyes off me, as if he doesn't want to miss a single bit of it.

I let out a breath, and with it, the shadows roll out of me. My arms change shape. My legs divide. Pincers grow out of me.

I feel myself grow. I get bigger. I feel more agile. My senses increase tenfold. And the pain dulls as the adrenaline of my darkling form takes over.

I turn my eyes to Jaxon as I complete the shift.

He's backed away across the bed, to the further side. I can see the fear in his eyes as he looks at me. But he isn't looking away. He isn't running.

"Does it hurt?" he asks as he looks me over. "When you…change…into…that?"

I shake my head. I prefer not to speak when I'm in this form. It's the one thing I don't care for about my true form. My voice sounds terrifying.

"How long can you stay like that for?" he asks. I see his hands flex into fists before releasing again. I remember then what I saw, when he fought with that guy he went to collect money from. Jaxon is deadly all on his own.

Not that he could stand a chance up against me right now. Not until he manifests.

I take a breath in, drawing in my shadows. My face returns to its usual form, my arms shrink, my legs return to normal. In a matter of two seconds, I'm just a woman sitting on the bed again.

I hiss in pain as it returns. "As long as I want," I answer his question.

Jaxon lets out a breath. I could hear how hard his heart was beating just a second ago. Thundering like a train racing down the tracks. He's still scared, but he looks more confident now that I look like the woman he met at the club again.

"You swear you're not out to kill me?" he asks.

I hold his gaze. "I swear. Like I said, I need you."

I think he's starting to believe me. It's evidenced by the fact that he didn't try to escape last night while I was sleeping. By the fact that he's not screaming for help outside our motel room door.

"We should get up and get ready to leave," I say. "We need to keep moving, less chance that ultralight will track us if we move on."

"Do I have time to take a shower?" Jaxon asks.

I almost smile. Who knows how long he's been awake. He could have showered whenever he wanted. This shows how afraid he really is. He waited until he could check with me. "Sure."

He climbs off the bed and without another word, heads into the bathroom and closes the door behind him.

I take thirty seconds to lie there in bed, staring at the place where he disappeared around the corner. Considering what little I know of him, I can't believe what's happening. He's obviously part of some crime family. He knows how to fight. He doesn't seem like one to be pushed around.

But he's doing whatever I say.

He's not trying to hurt me.

He's not freaking out.

Once more, my mind goes back to that night in the club, where our hands were all over each other, and the night was so natural and easy.

I'd dared to pretend for a little while, and it was so easy. I'd dared imagine that I could be with him.

Neither one of us would have imagined that it would lead to where we are right now.

I roll out of bed, throw back the window coverings, and let in the brilliantly blinding sunshine of morning.

Only then do I remember that I am only in my underwear and a bra.

I was all kinds of on display when Jaxon and I were talking just a moment ago.

I blush. And then shrug. Because there's nothing I can do to change that now.

I look around. This might be a hotel room, but we walked in with nothing but a few medical supplies. No changes of clothes, not even toothbrushes.

I pull my dirty clothes back on. I grab the thigh pack I slipped under my pillow, the one with my gun, and strap it back on.

I feel blind. I have no phone. I have no idea where the Kindred is. It's hard not to panic. I don't want to overreact, but I also don't want to underreact.

I need to get a new phone. Now. I need to get back in contact with the compound.

My head pops up when Jaxon steps out of the bathroom and steam rolls out behind him. He looks at me with wet hair, the stitches on his face still angry and prominent.

Every bit of me aches. He looks like every woman's

fantasy right now. Rugged, his long hair falling wet in his face.

*Get it together,* I scold myself. *He's an ultralight.*

"You ready?" I ask.

He just nods. So we head to the door, out into the blazing heat. I check out, crumpling the receipt in my hand. Together, we climb into our stolen car.

I start the engine, navigate us back to the freeway, and point us north.

I choose that direction, because the Kindred came from that way, and I don't know that he'll be too anxious to backtrack.

"Did you sleep?" I ask.

"A few minutes."

I would have been surprised if he had. Despite the insanity of the day, I actually fell asleep within minutes of my head hitting the pillow. I'd slept like the dead even though that was so stupid and dangerous.

"So what do you want me to start with?" I ask, knowing we might as well make use of our time on the road, completely uninterrupted.

"Why are we on the run?" Jaxon asks without having to hesitate and think about it. "Why did it seem like that guy was trying to kill us?"

I look ahead, down the desert road. "He actually wasn't trying to kill you, just me."

"From where I'm sitting, it kind of looked like he

was trying to get through you to get to me," Jaxon says doubtfully.

I shake my head. "Oh, he was trying to get through me, he would have ripped my head clean off if I would have let him. But he wouldn't have killed you." I rest my elbow against the window, lacing my fingers back into my hair. "But this isn't exactly where I want to be starting."

"You're the one who asked," he points out.

"I know," I say with a sigh at myself. "Okay, um. The DarkVerse. We can start there, sound good?"

"Okay," he agrees.

It's kind of throwing me off, how...calm he is. He seems like the last type of person who would come to terms with insane supernatural stuff like this.

"So most everything in the DarkVerse is the opposite of here. Here, everyone lives by the schedule of the sun. Awake during the day, asleep at night. You can see in the light, not the dark." Even now, I find myself squinting against the brightness of the sun. "In the DarkVerse, we live in the dark. We see in the dark. Even our plants and animals thrive in the dark. The sun is just...too much."

"But the DarkVerse isn't totally dark?" he asks for clarification.

I shake my head. "Just how there is darkness here, there is light there."

He doesn't say anything, just stares straight out the

window. He's being calm, but he is also exceptionally hard to read right now. I can't tell how he's processing this.

"The DarkVerse and the LightVerse, no one knows they exist?" he finally asks. "Other than the darklings and the ultralights?"

I nod. "Some information has to have gotten leaked somehow, there's just no other reason the parallel universe theory would exist. But no, we've all managed to keep it under tight wraps."

"But there's a way between the two verses?" Jaxon asks. From his tone, I can tell he thinks he sounds insane. Like he can't believe he's asking these questions, that we are having this conversation. But he's asking questions. "You said something about a gate."

I nod again. "The two verses intersect at one point. Don't go asking me where it is, that information is classified. But yes, they intersect."

"Then why don't you just…walk through it, or whatever, and go home?" he asks, looking over at me.

I give a sigh. This could take weeks to explain everything I've been trapped dealing with for the last century and a half. Some details are just going to slip my mind. "Because there's what's known as the gatekeeper. Just one ultralight born at a time who has the ability to open it. Both worlds would end if the gate just got left open between the verses."

"And that's what the darklings are looking for?" he

asks. "This ultralight who can open the gate? The darklings can't do it?"

"Yes, kind of," I say, tipping my head side to side. "That is what we're looking for. We check every ultralight who's about to manifest. We have been trying to track down the gatekeeper since we got stuck here. But no luck."

I try to recall the times I've traveled on this road. If I remember right, there's a town up ahead in about twenty minutes. St. George, Utah. It's big enough to have stores we can get supplies from, enough hotels we can move around for a few days if need be. I start watching for the exit signs.

"But it isn't just a one-sided thing," I say, continuing my explanation. "There's a gate on the DarkVerse side as well."

"There's a gatekeeper on that side too," Jaxon says, surprising me with how quickly he understands.

I nod. "So, it's not so simple as opening the gate on our side. None of this is simple."

I shake my head. It's all so much. There's just so much to explain, and how can I ever expect Jaxon to believe me?

"And like the parallel universe thing, whoever is on that side, the exact same person is on this side."

Jaxon's eyes snap to me. "You're saying we all have doppelgangers in the DarkVerse?"

Again, I'm surprised how quickly he's figuring

this out. I nod. "I'm saying there's another version, exactly like you, on the DarkVerse side. There was an exact version of me here on this side."

"Was?" Jaxon asks. "How do you know the light version of you is dead?"

I'm already tired. It's so much to explain, so much to try to make him understand. "I'm not in my own verse. This side doesn't even recognize my presence. Time doesn't work on me."

"You said you've been stuck for 158 years," Jaxon says, his voice trailing off.

"And I've been alive that entire time, stuck at the age of twenty-two," I say. I shake my head. I'm grateful for it. Better stuck at twenty-two than twelve or eighty-seven. There are worse things than being stuck in your prime.

Jaxon looks at me again. Like, really looks at me. Like he's looking for signs of wrinkles or needle pokes from Botox.

"Yeah, I know," I say, throwing a little sarcasm into my voice. "I look good for 180."

I didn't expect it, but he lets out a little laugh, looking out the window, shaking his head. And then he sits up at little straighter. "Wait, that's how you know your LightVerse version of yourself is dead. The ultra-lights are in their own verse. So, time recognizes them. They age?"

I nod. "They live a regular lifespan. They'll grow old and die when they're supposed to."

"So, you're immortal and that ultralight back there isn't," Jaxon says. With every question, with every explanation, I feel like his mind is opening up to what I'm saying.

"You got it," I say. "Though that doesn't mean I can't be killed. The ultralights have been picking us off one by one the entire time we've been trapped here." I swallow once. "We lost one of us just a few days ago."

"They're hunting you down?" he asks, regretful surprise in his tone.

I swallow once and nod.

Jaxon looks out the window again, and for a while he's quiet. And I'm grateful for a break. So I can process my grief. Deal with the fear I've been fixed with for 158 years. So I can sort out in my head everything else I still need to tell him.

I don't have to tell him anything. Really, maybe I shouldn't be telling him anything. He's going to be my enemy someday. We're naturally pitted against each other.

But what if this could do some good? None of us has exactly been friends with an ultralight. We've never ever been able to strike an understanding with one.

This is a unique situation.

What if we teach Jaxon about us? What if we can make him understand? What if he can change things?

I glance over at him. He's staring out the window, thinking, and something like hope surges in my veins.

Jaxon isn't the typical ultralight. He's…complex. Multi-faceted. He isn't strictly traditionally good or bad.

Maybe he could change things.

But will I ever get the other darklings to see the possibilities?

I see a sign for our exit, and I guide us off the freeway. I hook west down the road, and we don't have to roll very far before the mega store comes into view. I park close, it's still pretty quiet considering it's early on a Monday.

"Come on," I say. "I don't know about you, but I'm feeling a little disgusting in these clothes, and I'd really like to brush my teeth."

"You really think that no one is going to call the cops on us?" he asks, raising an eyebrow. "We look like we've been to hell and back, and murdered a few people on the way."

Looking down at us, he's right. There's blood and dirt and our clothes are ripped. "I don't see many other options," I say as I grip the door handle. "Come on."

We climb out of the car and walk into the store.

No one even seems to notice our presence. We don't get any strange looks. The two of us simply walk through the store, Jaxon pushing the cart.

"I have to say, you're handling this better than I expected," I say, looking over at him as I grab a two-pack of toothbrushes and toss them into the cart with the toothpaste. "After watching you for a day, I would have thought you'd be trying to kill me instantly. Or that you'd be calling your family to come murder me. Why aren't you reacting the way any normal human being would?"

"Well, one," Jaxon says as we navigate through the toiletries, grabbing what we need. "Sounds like you think I'm not fully human."

He looks over at me, and I can see it in his eyes, this does all still sound and feel crazy to him.

"Two. Call it morbid fascination." He glances over at me, and I see something new on his face. I see… longing. Desire. "I had the best night of my life, with the most beautiful woman I've ever seen. And then you started stalking me and erupted back into my life. I never thought I was going to get to see you again. Seems like a sick twist of fate that I'm getting this second chance."

My heart thunders. Because he just made a very honest confession.

I'd had the best night of my life too, when we were together in the club. I'd watched with so much regret when he left.

But here we are, together, under insane circumstances.

From the look on his face, I think Jaxon can read in my eyes that I feel the same way.

"And three, and this is kind of the biggest one," he says, grabbing a bottle of shampoo. "I saw it with my own eyes. I don't do drugs like my brother. I don't even drink. So, I can say with absolute certainty that I was sober when you stalked me down to that cemetery and shifted into this thing somewhere between a scorpion and smoke and the Mind Flayer. It's kind of hard to deny something when you've seen it with your own eyes."

Wow. I've never heard a more accurate description of what my darkling form looks like.

"Okay, sure, you saw it," I say. "But, I mean, I practically kidnapped you. I know you've got a whole life waiting for you back in Vegas. You have family that is undoubtedly looking for you. And I just snatched you out of it and dumped all this insane information on you. And now you're just…shopping with me like we're just two regular people?"

Jaxon looks over at me as we walk, headed for the underwear section. "I don't know." I can tell he means that. "I guess I should be a little more freaked out by you kidnapping me. I mean, I still don't even know your name."

Something like guilt drops in my stomach. He'd whispered his name in my ear at the club, and it had felt so intimate. I'd felt a connection in that moment.

But he'd asked me for my name after that, and I'd just ignored it, because I knew it couldn't continue beyond that night.

Yet here we were.

"Serena," I offer in a blurt. "My name is Serena."

We stop next to an endless row of men's underwear. I see this…look come into Jaxon's eyes. It's a little hungry. It's a little possessive. It's a little mischievous. "Well, it's nice to meet you, Serena."

I smirk, and just watch as he grabs a six pack and tosses it into the cart.

"Did you ever catch up to your brother that night?" I ask.

Jaxon grabs a black pair of jeans and throws them in the cart. "Yeah. I didn't give him much of a choice. I got him home. He wasn't exactly happy about it."

"You take care of your family often?" I ask, looking over at him. I know the answer before he gives it.

Jaxon shrugs. "You could say I come from a family of adrenaline junkies. They don't all have the most level heads." And he leaves it at that.

We head to the women's section, and I pick out some items to get me by until we can go back to Vegas.

Food is in order next. We get a lot of that. Apparently, we're both starving.

And just before we check out, I grab a phone. It's one of those pre-paid types. It's simple and dated, but it can make calls and receive texts. It will get me back in touch with the compound.

We check out, all paid for by the cash in Jaxon's wallet, and then head down the road.

"We should switch cars," Jaxon says. "Someone has probably reported this one stolen. We should ditch it and get another."

I glance over at him, and yet again, I'm wondering how he is an ultralight.

But he isn't wrong.

I turn left down a street, and we drive for five minutes through the suburbs, until the houses start stretching farther apart.

"Watch for security cameras," Jaxon says as we slowly roll through the neighborhood. The houses get older. We need an older car. One that isn't stuck in a garage. "Doesn't help if someone catches us with their doorbell camera."

And there we find the perfect target. There is a house at the end of the street. On the curb, there is a car parked, something similar to this one. Older, small. We both scan the houses around, but none of them have cameras, at least, not ones we can see, and they don't seem like the kind of houses to have hidden cameras.

"I'll get it started," Jaxon says as I stop next to it. "You drive back a few blocks and we'll ditch it in the parking lot and get in."

I consider it for a second. He could run. With a car, he might have a chance of outrunning me.

But he didn't run last night.

And I know he wants more answers.

"Okay," I say, deciding to trust him, against my better judgement.

He climbs out of the car and looks around as he walks to the driver's door of our targeted vehicle. He must not see anything too worrisome, because he pulls on the door, and it's just our luck when it's unlocked.

I watch him reach under the dashboard, and not seven seconds later, I hear it roar to life.

My insides half shift as I watch him pull away from the curb. If he hits the gas too hard, I will shift fully and burst from the car and overtake it before he can get very far. I'll risk exposure, being seen, but it's better than him getting away and another ultralight finding him before we can test him.

But he drives the speed limit. He goes back down the street and turns right, heading for the parking lot we talked about. He parks in a stall and I pull up right next to him.

I breathe a sigh of relief as he climbs out and pops the trunk.

Neither of us says a word as we unload all our things from my trunk into his. We do it quickly, because there might be cameras in this parking lot that might be able to see our faces and license plates.

We're back in the seats of the car in less than sixty seconds.

Jaxon gets back in the driver's seat and I drop into the passenger, and we're once more pulling out onto the road.

"Where do you want to head?" he asks. "I've got about 150 left in my wallet. If we go cheap, we'll be able to get two more nights somewhere."

I swear under my breath. I don't know if that's enough. But we have no other options. "There's another town just north of this one. Kind of a retirement community. I'm pretty sure there's a hotel there."

Jaxon just nods and navigates us back to the freeway.

I use this time to get my burner phone set up. I put the chip in and call in to get it activated. And then, one by one, I recall my crew's phone numbers and enter them in.

My heart races though when I get it all good to go. I need to call. They'll be panicking that I might be dead. They'll be tracking Jaxon through the system, but they won't risk going after him until they hear from me, because if that Kindred is anywhere near us, it will be too dangerous.

"You going to call your people?" Jaxon asks as he looks over at me.

I take a second to answer. My heart is racing and my palms feel slick. "It's going to be complicated.

They're not going to be happy that we're on the run. They'll want to test you as soon as possible."

I don't know why, but Jaxon doesn't question any of that. He simply gives an acknowledging sound, and nods.

I should be worried about him. What he does, his family, his reactions, I know there is some shade behind Jaxon.

Instead, I feel that thread of connection that started forming between us that night growing just a little thicker. I feel the knot around my heart cinching a little tighter.

I tell him when we reach the exit, and we navigate off the freeway. We pull into the parking lot of the hotel and I look at the time. "Check in probably isn't for a few more hours."

"It's a Monday," Jaxon says as he looks around the parking lot. "Everyone probably checked out yesterday morning. There probably aren't many checking in today. Doesn't hurt to ask if they have a room ready now."

So we both climb out, and despite our rough appearance, we walk into the lobby.

The man working there looks at us warily, but Jaxon smoothly offers an apology and a story about how we were in a car accident on our way from Salt Lake to Vegas. Our car is in the shop and we're stuck here until it's fixed.

The man buys it and looks at us with sympathy instead of suspicion. Jaxon flashes a fake ID, registers us under a fake name. The clerk slides two room keys across the counter after Jaxon pays him in cash for one night.

"You're an exceptionally good liar," I observe as we walk back out to the car for our supplies.

"I imagine you aren't too bad at it either, considering you're a darkling who's been hiding in the wrong world for a century and a half," he jabs right back as we close the trunk and head for the back stairs.

"Touché," I admit with a smirk.

We climb up to the third floor and walk down three doors before reaching our room number. Jaxon swipes the card, and we step inside.

We both stop in the doorway when we take in the room, and note that there is only one king-sized bed.

"You did make it sound like we were a couple," I say, looking over at him.

"I can keep to my side if you keep to yours," he says. But the tiny smirk that pulls on one side of his mouth gives away what's really going through his head.

I can't help that a little one pulls on my mouth as well.

## Chapter Six

We step inside and set our things down on the desk.

"You get ready and changed first," I say. "I need to make the call."

Jaxon just nods, digs through the bags for his things, and steps into the bathroom.

I stand in front of the window. It looks out over the desert, the orange rock landscape around us. It looks pretty similar to home.

I shake my head.

Nope. Not home. Just where I've been stuck for eighty percent of my existence.

I open the contacts and scroll down to Davorian's number and hit call.

It rings twice before he answers.

"Hello?" he asks warily.

"It's me," I say simply.

"Thank the dark," he says in a huff. "We thought you might be dead."

"I know," I say with a nod, even though he can't see it. "I'm sorry. We ran into a Kindred and during the scuffle, my phone got wrecked. I didn't get a chance to get a new one until just now."

"You say we," Davorian says. "I assume that means you're still with the ultralight?"

I look back at the bathroom door. I can hear the shower running and see steam already leaking out from beneath it. "Yeah," I answer. "He's not what I expected. But he's taking this all…better than expected. And he's not trying to run. I don't think I'm going to have any trouble bringing him back to the compound."

"Well, I think you're going to have to wait until tomorrow to come back," Davorian says. I imagine him looking around the compound or pacing. He's always so restless. "I don't know what the timing of it all is, but Renwick tracked him down on the Strip a few hours before dawn."

"That would have been right after I hit the road with Jaxon," I say, clearing up the timeline.

Davorian pauses a moment, and it takes me a second to realize why. I called him Jaxon, a personal name, instead of the ultralight. "Well, Renwick and Philomena have been chasing the Kindred all over the area. Last update I heard they had him cornered in the

Grand Canyon. I expect to hear back from them as soon as the threat has been eliminated."

A knot forms in my throat. Because just a few days ago, we got word that one of us was dead, and that was at the hand of this same Kindred.

I just have to have a little faith. Philomena and Renwick are some of the very best.

"Alright," I say, pushing aside my worry. "Let me know when it's clear to come back. We'll hang low until I get word."

"Stay safe, Serena," Davorian says, and he ends the call.

I look down at my phone when the call is over. My brain is hundreds of miles away, in the Grand Canyon, picturing the epic fight that must be going on right now. Two darklings up against one ultralight, I should feel confident in the numbers. But the Kindred are ruthless.

"Everything okay?"

I look up at the sound of Jaxon's voice.

He stands there across the room, dressed in fresh jeans and a black t-shirt. His wet hair has been brushed back from his face. But that's genuine concern and worry in his dark eyes.

"My comrades have chased the Kindred to the Grand Canyon," I say around a thick throat. "It's two against one. But still. He killed one of our own just a few days ago. I'm just worried about my friends."

Jaxon holds my eyes for a long moment, and I can tell he doesn't know what to say. He doesn't know me. He doesn't know them. He doesn't even know what half of what I just said meant.

"The water pressure is good in there," he says. "Plenty hot. Maybe a shower will help. And then I have some more questions. If you're feeling up to it."

I simply shake my head, my brows furrowing.

Jaxon makes no sense.

But I don't say anything. I cross the room, grab some clothes from our shopping bags, and head into the shower.

It does help. I might have gotten clean last night, but going straight back into my dirty and blood caked clothes left me feeling disgusting. I stand in the line of the hot water for a long time, letting it wash away everything.

I'm scared. So scared. And that's not something I feel very often.

Over the past 158 years, I've allowed myself to let go of any emotions. Except maybe anger. That, I held onto as a defense. But I've let hope fizzle the last few decades. I haven't felt joy in more than a century. I even had to let panic and despair go.

But right now, it's fear that I have to ignore.

Things are out of my hands for the moment. So, I need to just be here, in this moment, handling what I can.

When I'm done washing my hair, I turn off the water and dry off. I pull on the black jeans I got and slip on the black tank top I got to go with it. I brush out my hair, and stare at myself in the mirror.

I look tired. I am tired.

But still, I step out of the bathroom.

Jaxon is standing at the window, the spot that I occupied just twenty minutes ago. He stares out over the desert landscape, and I wonder what's going through his head.

"If you take me back to this gate, and I'm not this gatekeeper, what happens then?" Jaxon asks without looking at me.

I swallow once. This answer should be easy. It shouldn't make something in my chest ache. It shouldn't make me think of that night at the club. "We'll let you go, and you'll manifest. And you will get to choose what kind of life you'll have. But it won't be the same as before."

"Why?" he asks as he looks back at me.

I climb up into the bed. My whole body still aches. I'm covered in bruises. The burn marks are still fresh and prominent. With a hiss of pain, I scoot back and prop my back against a pillow. "Because when this universe was created, it was created with one fatal flaw."

I can tell from the look in his eyes that I've caught his attention. He turns and walks to the desk pushed against the wall. He pulls the chair out, spins it around. He sits and props his bare feet up on the edge of the bed.

"The gate itself shouldn't exist," I say. "There is no logical reason for it. Nothing good happens from a portal being open between our verses. We have always believed it to be a mistake. But the bigger problem is that where our two worlds intersect, there is this… energy that is created."

Goosebumps flash across my skin just thinking about it. I can remember my encounters in the Dark-Verse, when the hair on my body would stand on end, and this tingle would creep up my scalp. My shadow being would instantly surge, ready to burst forth.

"This energy is imbalanced, being claimed neither by the LightVerse or the DarkVerse, and it can travel to either. This energy, it wants to attach itself to a host, to something living."

I see goosebumps wash over Jaxon's arms, and his eyes narrow. This is creeping him out, and I don't blame him.

"Sometimes it's an animal," I continue. "And this energy takes over. Like, have you ever heard of a dog that's always been a good dog, but it suddenly just…snaps?"

Jaxon doesn't say anything, but I can tell he knows exactly what I'm talking about.

"But usually it's a person that it attaches to," I say,

and I hate the words. "I'm sure you've heard of posses-sion, and that's exactly what it's like. A person will suddenly act very different. They'll be filled with this…darkness."

My eyes rise up to the ceiling and I recall the first time I came across this. Shivers ran over my entire body and it was as if a wailing alarm was going off in my soul.

"It's called the Dusk," I say. "Because it's a result of neither light nor dark. The darklings and the ultralights evolved as a result of it. It's the reason we exist, to protect humankind from it, and to expel it from those who are possessed."

"Are you telling me your entire reason for existing is to perform exorcisms?" Jaxon asks, his voice tight.

My eyes slide back over to meet his. "Yes," I answer.

He swallows once, and he looks a little paler.

"Once you manifest, you'll be able to sense the Dusk," I say. "Sometimes you can tell before, even. Anyone can occasionally. Have you ever been around someone, and they just feel…dark? Wrong?"

The look in his eyes tells me yes.

I nod. "There are two ways this happens. A simple possession can be exorcised by an ultralight. But some-times, the host embraces the Dusk."

A shiver makes its way through my entire body. The feeling that courses through my being when I encountered them…it was like cold blindness took over.

"Once the host embraces the Dusk, it can't be expelled. Usually, the host is so far gone, you have no choice but to destroy them."

"You mean kill them?" Jaxon asks, hard doubt in his voice.

I nod.

"Doesn't that seem wrong?" Jaxon questions. "They didn't ask to be possessed. There has to be a chance they'll change. How do you justify taking their life?"

"Trust me," I say. "If they've embraced the Dusk, you'll understand. You'll see that there is no other choice."

It would happen. The time would come. And he would understand.

"How often does it happen?" Jaxon asks, his voice slightly hoarse. "When was the last time you had to destroy one?"

I sit up a little straighter. "About 158 years," I answer. "I'm not a guardian of this verse. I can't sense the Dusk here. Only the ultralights can."

He takes a second to digest that. "And the ultralights, we, what? Team up to perform these exorcisms?"

I shake my head. "Not exactly. It's different here. In the DarkVerse, the darklings are, or at least were, very organized. We train. We have ranks. But the ultralights haven't been organized since the war. Not since they lost their commander. Now, they generally work on their own, and most aren't even aware there are other ultralights out there. The just do what they can't help but do. Except for the Kindred."

His eyes light up a bit. "You've said that word before. That's what you called that guy that tried to kill you."

I nod. "The Kindred formed within a year or so of the gate closing, when we got marooned here. They're…radicals. They don't care so much about eliminating the Dusk. Their organization exists to find the darklings in the LightVerse, and eliminate them."

"They're hunting you?" Jaxon says. His tone hardens and his eyes narrow.

I nod. "When the gate closed, there were over five hundred of us stranded here. Now, there are only about fifty of us left."

I shouldn't be telling him this. This is classified information that he could somehow possibly use against us in the future.

But I just keep talking.

Maybe this is a coping mechanism. After so long being trapped here, I kind of feel like it's not real. That I'm going insane. I'm starting to forget my own world and how I got here and why I'm fighting so hard to find the gatekeeper.

Saying it all, telling it to someone else, it makes it real once more.

"One by one, the Kindred are hunting us down. They're highly trained, the most advanced of the ultralights, because they are the only ones who band together. Don't get me wrong. We've killed plenty of them defending ourselves, to survive, but they've had over 150 years to hunt us down. It's an ever-shrinking pool."

"Why?" Jaxon asks. "Why do they want to kill you so bad? What did the darklings ever do to them?"

I meet his eyes. "It's not about what was done. It's about nature and instinct. Our kind, your kind, we evolved to be guardians of our verses. We evolved to eliminate things that don't belong. And once you manifest, you won't be able to help it. Your every instinct is going to be to kill me."

He doesn't say anything. I can practically see the gears turning in his head. His eyes drift down from mine, searching all of me, as if he's testing himself out for any instinct inside of him to hurt me.

"So we need to hurry this up," Jaxon says. "We need to test me at this gate, and then I need to get far away from you. And your kind."

"Basically," I say with a hoarse voice. "But trust me, I can defend myself. Especially against a newborn ultralight. But I don't want to hurt you either."

We both stare at each other, and I wonder if there's

an ache in his chest as well. Does he also feel like this is unfair? Because I can't deny it, there is something awake in my chest that hasn't been awake in over a hundred years.

"That's enough," Jaxon says as he stands up. "My brain can't take any more today. I need to eat something, or I am going to starve to death."

I give a little huff of a laugh. He's right. We need to eat something. We haven't eaten anything all day, we've been on the run for eighteen hours. We've eaten nothing since then.

It's an oddly comfortable time, the next hour that we spend together. We put together a simple meal, nothing that has to be cooked because we don't have an oven or stove. But we cobble something suitable together. Neither of us says much of anything at all. Jaxon has so much to process. I still can't believe that he doesn't think he's gone crazy, or that I'm crazy, or maybe that I even drugged him at the club, and he's been on a constant trip since then. So, I give him his time and his space to think over everything that I've said.

By the time we're both finished eating, it's dark outside. I feel as if we haven't done enough today, it was a shopping spree, a drive, and then we've just been sitting here inside of this hotel room, waiting for word that it's safe to return to Las Vegas.

But the day has been so long. I'm actually relieved

when Jaxon reaches for the remote and turns the TV on. He flips through a few channels before he stops on some movie. It's an old one, one I've seen before. But it's actually nice, because it's mindless. It directs my eyes, but my brain doesn't have to stay focused on it to understand what's going on.

It was awkward for all of three seconds. I was already lying on the bed when Jaxon turned the TV on. After he picked a channel, he looked at me lying on the bed for just a few moments and I could see him considering if this was okay or not. Everything else in his and our world was completely off kilter, so he simply climbed into the bed next to me, bunched up a pillow beneath his head, and watched the television.

## Chapter Seven

I DON'T REMEMBER FALLING asleep, but I also can't remember much of the movie at all. When my eyes slide open, there is already plenty of sunlight coming in from behind the blackout curtains. I'm lying on my side, facing away from the window. Before I even open my eyes, I can sense the warmth beside me. And for a moment, I don't want to break this moment that I know cannot last. I take a breath in, taking note of every scent that comes off his body. I take stock of the level of comfort I feel in this moment. I am warm, the bed is comfortable. In this very second, there is nothing pressing for our attention. There is nothing dire.

I can feel something soft but firm beneath my arm, and feel something else on top of that same arm that is equally heavy and warm. Slowly, I let my eyes open. My hand is lying on top of Jaxon's, and his other hand is lying on top of that arm. It almost looks as if we have been holding hands the entire night.

His face is not far from mine, and he's still dead asleep. He looks younger when he sleeps. More innocent. More like the ultralight he is meant to be. As if the weight of the way he has grown up doesn't exist. He almost looks like anyone in the world who had something that could be considered a normal life.

Neither of us has any clue what normal really is. Our lives have been so different, but yet at the same time they have both been filled with the uncertain, stress, and the fight for survival.

I know why I keep thinking back to that night at the club. The both of us were pretending our lives were not what they were. We were both living in a fantasy, wishing with everything we had that what happened that night was real. We were both living in the moment.

So I tell myself to appreciate one more moment. This one is stolen, just like that other one. It might not have had the heat and excitement that the club did, Jaxon's hands on my hips, my hands behind his neck pulling him close. This was something different. This feels…real. After 158 years of observation of the LightVerses' world, I think I have a fairly good inclination of what normal life is supposed to look like.

This kind of looks normal to me.

But as Jaxon's eyes flutter open, I know the truth.

We do not belong to each other. We have only known each other for a matter of days. And in another matter of days, we will go our separate ways and we will never see each other again. We are exact opposites, something evolutionary.

So, I need to be careful.

"Morning," Jaxon says. He searches my face, and I don't doubt that he's having his own internal debate about what is okay and what is real.

"Morning," I say as I roll over and stand from the bed. I head to the bathroom and close the door behind me. I take care of things, and step back out.

"Your phone just buzzed," Jaxon says as he looks over at it, sitting on the nightstand on my side of the bed.

I quickly cross the room to it, snatching it off the nightstand.

*The coast is clear, Philomena and Renwick took care of the problem. You can come back to the compound.*

"Looks like we can go home," I say as my eyes rise up to meet Jaxon's.

Just then, there is a heavy knock on the door.

Both my head and Jaxon's pop up, our eyes snapping to the door. My heart rate instantly doubles, and I scramble to reach for my hip pack, pulling my handgun out. When Jaxon takes a step for the door, I hold one finger up, signaling for him to wait. I silently creep forward, walking to the door, my eyes fixed on the peephole.

There's a very distinct, loud ring of metal being struck by metal. I hear the sound of a silencer, and absolutely recognize the sound of a shot being fired at the door handle.

I whip around, getting ready to shift, even as I am grabbing Jaxon, and aim for the window. Just as the door is kicked in, I turn, half a second from throwing us through the window. I raise the handgun, aiming it at the door.

I couldn't afford to hesitate. There was not time to consider if I should have fired the gun or not. I had to protect Jaxon, and myself, at all costs.

My bullet strikes a shoulder, just as two figures burst into the room.

My brain can't quite make sense of what I'm seeing. I was expecting a glowing ultralight, a Kindred here to take Jaxon, and kill me.

Instead, I see familiar green eyes, I see familiar dirty blond hair, and the hard faces of a family I have seen before.

But I fired first, and my arms are around Jaxon, like I am about to leap from the window. Which I was in fact about to do.

One of Jaxon's brothers raises a gun and fires a shot. It misses the edge of my head, but just barely. It embeds itself into the wall beside me. Every single gun raised has a silencer on it so the only one that made any noise was mine.

We probably have about five minutes before cops show up. There's no way the desk attendant is going to come running up here considering the sound of gunfire was unmistakable. And hopefully any other guests in this hotel are smart enough to stay in their rooms.

"Whoa, whoa, whoa!" Jaxon yells, holding both of his hands up, and backing me up toward a wall. My finger is on the trigger, aimed at one brother, and then the next. Adrenaline is surging through my blood, and my darkling form is one breath away from escaping. "What the hell are you guys doing here? And what's with the guns?"

The oldest one, the one with the Viking beard, steps forward, his eyes fixed on me. There is death in his eyes, revenge and blood. "You go missing instantly at our brother's funeral, that sounds like the declaration of a blood war. She's got something to do with AJ's death, doesn't she? What family are you from? The Corderos? The Lawrences?"

"You thought I was kidnapped?" Jaxon says, defense, annoyance, and amusement heavy in his voice. "Come on Blake, you think any of the Corderos could have taken me against my will?"

"You disappeared," another of Jaxon's brothers says. "Your phone was left in Vegas. The man who killed AJ is still at large. Are you seriously trying to tell me that she has nothing to do with this? Look at her! She's two seconds away from shooting you herself."

He's wrong. My gun is still fully fixed right at his head.

Jaxon reaches up, and pats me on the arm, which is tightly clasped around his shoulders. It's a signal, to let him go so he can deal with the situation. It takes everything I have in me to let him go.

Jaxon takes four aggressive steps across the hotel room and sharply grabs the oldest brother by the front of his shirt. He slams him back against the closet wall. "I am not a prisoner, Blake," Jaxon says between gritted teeth. "I did my work for the week. What I do with my weekend off is none of your business."

"You trying to tell me you willingly came here with her? That this…" he waves his gun between Jaxon and I, "this was just some fling?"

"What the hell does it look like?" Jaxon grits out. His tone gets angrier and angrier by the moment. "We met at the club the other day. After all that heaviness with AJ, I might've needed a little bit of a release. I think you of all people would understand, Griff."

Slowly, the darkling inside of me relaxes. Jaxon lies to his brothers as easily as he breathes. And his story is a convincing one.

"She just shot me," Griff says as he looks down at

his bleeding shoulder. "Is this the kind woman you're sleeping with these days?"

"You're the one who burst in here with a gun pointed in her face," Jaxon says with a bit of a smirk. He finally lets Blake go and takes a step away from him, back toward me.

"Sorry," I say, my tone definitely implying that I am not sorry. "I tend to be a shoot first, ask questions later, type of person."

That crooks a smile on Blake's face. "You know how to pick them, Jaxon. I think she'll fit in just fine."

"How did you even find us?" Jaxon asks. But he immediately shakes his head. "No, never mind. I don't want to know."

Jaxon walks to my side, his hands resting on his hips. He glares darkly at his brothers, but I can tell the danger is over. He's diffused the situation. So, I lower my gun, and holster it back in my hip pack.

"Now that you can see I haven't been kidnapped, you can let yourself back out the door. We need a minute to clear out of here before the cops show up. Thanks for ruining my weekend."

He genuinely sounds annoyed. I actually believe that he's upset his brothers burst in and interrupted all this private space we've had.

Blake smirks and nods his head. "Mom wants you back by Saturday. Sounds like there's going to be an issue you might need to take care of. Get your brass knuckles ready."

Blake steps towards the door, holstering his gun at his hip. Griff looks at us with a smirk, and I don't much like the look in his eyes. "Have fun. Use protection."

They walk out of sight, and I hear the sounds of their footsteps as they go down the back stairs.

"Grab your stuff," Jaxon says as he bursts to a flurry of activity. Instantly, he's grabbing everything within sight, shoving it all into the grocery bags we got from the store. I don't hesitate. I feel like there's something that I should be saying, that I should be questioning his family and everything that just happened. But I'm not surprised by it. I saw what I saw the night I followed him. A killing. A funeral in the middle of the night. Blood and gore. I knew what to expect, so, what is there to say? His family is what it is. Jaxon didn't get to pick them.

So I set to gathering all of our things from the hotel room. I clear out the bathroom, stuffing everything into one of the grocery bags. We retrieve all the food we had, packing it into the bags as well. I grab my burner phone from the charger and stuff it into my pocket.

Only sixty seconds after Jaxon's brothers left, he and I head out into the hall, leaving the hotel room keys on the dresser. At a quick pace, we walk down the hall and exit out the back door. Jaxon pops the trunk, and we shove our bags into it. I don't give him a choice, I take the driver seat and close the door behind me. We peel out of the parking lot and I make my way onto the freeway. Just as we've merged onto it, I hear the wail of sirens and then see the red and blue flashes of lights as the police cars pull into the parking lot of the hotel.

Jaxon leans back in his seat, letting out a huff of air. This might be his life, but it's obvious it still causes him stress.

"My life was never boring before," he says. "I didn't think I needed any more adrenaline spikes, but then you came into it and it's been a nonstop rush ever since."

"I wish I could say things were going to calm down from here," I say as I focus on the road ahead. "But that's never going to be the case again."

I dig into my pocket and pull my burner phone out. I glance down at it, taking my eyes from the road for just a few moments as I scroll through the contacts on my phone. I click on Ascelin's name and hold it to my ear.

He answers just three seconds later. "That you?"

"Yeah," I say. "Just a heads up, I'm on my way back to the compound with the target. So don't freak out when two specks show up on your screens."

"How long?"

We pass a sign just then, one that says we're 120 miles from Las Vegas. "Maybe an hour and fifteen minutes."

Jaxon makes a chuckle then, shaking his head. We're only going to reach Las Vegas in one hour if I floor it. Which I do in that moment.

"Thanks for the heads up," Ascelin says. "I'll make sure I don't shoot you down when you get here."

I chuckle and end the call.

"Sounds like you guys have some heavy-duty security there," Jaxon says.

"We have pretty advanced scanners," I say. "Ascelin is in charge of security. But for the most part the darklings are security enough. We're well armed, but even without weapons, we can defend ourselves."

Jaxon simply nods and looks out at the desert landscape around us.

"Has your family always been like that?" I ask as I glance over at him. "Has it always been guns blazing and broken doors?"

He takes a second to answer and I wonder if I've stumbled into a sensitive topic. But when he speaks, it's simple statements of fact. "My mother grew up in this life. It's all she ever knew. Her father trained her in the business, and she inherited it at the age of eighteen when he was shot down. She's good at what she does. She handles people who don't pay up on their gambling debts. Trust me, she won't hesitate in beating you to death, after she's cut your fingers off."

I think back to my own mother and it makes me ache for Jaxon that our childhoods were so vastly different.

"My mother got bored of lovers quickly," Jaxon continues. "Blake's dad was a guy she met at a bar in the casino she was operating in back then. She kept him around for the first six months of the pregnancy but when he got on her nerves one night, she sent one of her henchmen after him. He was never seen again. Aaron and Griff have the same dad. He was the one that lasted the longest. I think maybe she even might have loved him. But when she caught him cheating, there were multiple pieces of him found scattered throughout the city."

Goosebumps flash over my skin. I can hardly even picture it, a woman with all these children, yet performing all these deadly acts.

"My sister Chantel, she's just older than I am, her dad actually got out. He'd had enough and when Chantel was just six days old, he took off and no one's heard from him since." Jaxon rubs two fingers over his lips looking thoughtfully outside. "My dad's actually still alive. Though he has no idea that I exist. He and my mom had a one-night stand and by that point, I think she was getting a little tired of taking care of lovers. She simply didn't tell him. He was another shylock in Vegas but then for some reason, he up and moved out of the city eight years ago. He was in New York City for a while, but I lost track of him three years ago."

I've wondered at Jaxon's father. Could he actually have been a good man, is being good in Jaxon's veins? In his blood? I had my doubts considering all the other family history Jaxon was telling me about.

"Scarlett comes next, she's eighteen. Her dad was a male stripper who used to come to the casino all the time. Mom liked to look at him, so she kept him around. Apparently, she didn't just look. He kept coming around, he seemed to think he was in love with my mother. Poor bastard had no idea what he was really getting into. She got tired of him following her around like a love-sick puppy so she put him on her collections team. He got himself shot within the first week of work."

I feel like I've already lost track of how many bodies Jaxon's mother has dropped, and we weren't even to the end of it yet.

"Mom isn't sure who AJ's dad was," I hear Jaxon's voice get tighter when he says his youngest brother's name. "Apparently it could've been one of a couple of guys. Which is probably lucky, it probably saved a life that she has no idea who it really is. By that point she didn't really care anymore, I think she was getting sick of offing so many men."

Jaxon is quiet after that. He looks out the window and I can already tell that his mind is 100 miles away.

"I'm really sorry about your brother," I offer with a sympathetic tone. "I saw it happen. I know you tried to convince your family that he was too young to go out. You were right. You're a good brother for trying to protect him and standing up to your family for him."

Jaxon clears his throat, but he doesn't look back at me. "I had these dreams that one of us might get out. When it didn't happen for Scarlett I tried really, really hard to keep AJ out of this. But Mom wouldn't have that. Neither would Blake, and he is her second in command. Never hated saying *I told you so,* so much."

He continues staring out the window and I can tell he's trying to keep it together in this moment.

He hasn't had any time to really mourn his brother. AJ was shot, Jaxon took him to the doctor, who pronounced him dead, and within two hours, his brother was already in the ground. And then I snatched him straight from the funeral into all of this insanity.

Jaxon needs time to mourn his brother, and the only time he is going to get is whatever time is left between here and the compound.

I stay quiet after that. Jaxon doesn't say anything else. Silently, I watch the landscape fly by as I press harder and harder on the gas pedal.

## Chapter Eight

THREE MILES out from the exit, I reach into the back seat and grab a t-shirt.

"Put this over your eyes," I say.

"Excuse me?" Jaxon asks, looking over at me with narrowed eyes.

I give a sigh. "Look, you're going to be an ultralight in a matter of days. Like I said, we'll be mortal enemies then. I can't have you knowing exactly where the compound is."

From the look in his eyes, I can tell that he doesn't love this. He lets out an annoyed sigh, but he takes the shirt and ties it around his eyes.

I hope that I can trust he can't see.

"How much longer?" he asks as he sits there, blindfolded.

"We'll be off the freeway soon," I say, even as I see the exit approaching.

I pull off and head under the overpass. We point out at the desert, and I accelerate.

We drive. And drive. The pavement ends, and our tires hit dirt.

I drive a little longer. And then I put the car into park.

"That was closer than I expected," Jaxon says.

"We're not there yet. We walk from here," I say as I open my door and climb out. I walk around to his side and pull his door open. "This car is stolen. I can't risk driving it right up to the compound."

"You want me to walk through the desert," Jaxon asks dubiously. "Blindfolded."

I reach forward and grab his hand. "Just trust me."

He's quiet as we take our first steps. I can tell he's thinking over my request.

Does he trust me?

I ignore the electricity that is racing through my blood. I am absolutely aware of every point that our skin is touching. I can feel him beside me with every instinct in me.

*Stop,* I tell myself. *He's going to try to kill you in a few days. You might kill him in self-defense.*

So, I focus on the path ahead.

We have nearly two miles ahead of us. Two miles of dry desert, dust, and sandstone.

And then it's a maze of rocks and hills. It's an endless landscape of red and pink and white. While I may resent it with every ounce of my being, there is a certain beauty in the desert. It's so tough and relentless. It will still be here long after humans die off.

My heart races when I finally spot the rocks that hide the entrance.

I know what's waiting for us down beneath the surface.

"It's going to be dark," I say in warning. "We don't need light, but there is plenty of secondary light. Your eyes will eventually adjust. But you're probably going to feel blind for a few minutes."

"'K." Finally, I hear nerves in Jaxon's voice. His throat is tight, and the word comes out rough.

"And I'm going to have to shift to get us in," I say, my heart rate picking up even more. "You're going to feel me grabbing you, and it's going to be…my darkling form. So, don't freak out, okay?"

Jaxon swallows, and I watch his Adam's apple bob up and down. He simply nods.

We take the last five steps, and I stop there, the entrance hole right at our feet.

I can feel my darkling form just under the surface. It's been on the edge, so ready to take over, for days now.

It is the easiest shift in the world when I let it take over.

My blood dissolves into shadows and smoke. My limbs separate and multiply. My jaw changes shape. I have claws instead of feet.

It's like a breath of relief.

I love my darkling form.

But still, I'm so nervous when I turn back to Jaxon. He's pale and I swear his hands shake just a little bit as he waits.

"Ready?" I ask and hate the way my voice sounds. Like a sonic demon.

Jaxon just gives one stiff nod.

I grab him with four arms, picking him up carefully. He flinches, hard, and he takes in a sharp breath. But he doesn't try to squirm away.

So, I take the plunge, eager to get this over with as quickly as possible. With my free legs, I climb down into the hole. I skitter through the twists and turns, all the while being careful not to jostle Jaxon too much.

It grows darker as I descend, and everything in me is so aware of it. I feel my body relaxing into the dark, into my natural state. It envelops me with comfort.

And finally, I hit the ground floor.

I shift not one second later, setting Jaxon on his feet even as I shift back into human form.

I can hear the others coming down the hall. I don't want Jaxon to be bombarded, to have them be the first thing he sees, so I quickly reach over and pull the blindfold from his eyes.

He blinks four times fast when it's removed. His eyes immediately search for me, and he takes one quick scan up and down me to see if I'm a darkling or human. When he sees what I am, he turns his gaze to the rest of what is before him.

He's seeing a long hallway with rooms that branch off of it. There are lights blinking from different pieces of equipment. I can see the glow of multiple screens down the hall.

And then four figures step into view, walking down the hall.

For a few seconds, the instinct to step in front of Jaxon and protect him rips through me. It's so strong I find myself curling my hands into fists.

But that's ridiculous. These are my people. My family. I don't need to protect Jaxon from them.

It's Ascelin who walks at the head, and I guess I shouldn't be surprised by that. He's head of security. And even though that means he's usually stuck here in the compound, he is unquestionably the best fighter of us all. He was a teacher at the Academy. Back home.

His expression is hard, and his eyes are fixed directly on Jaxon. If looks could kill, Jaxon would at least be paralyzed.

He's followed immediately by Philomena, and then Renwick.

Philomena's expression is dead serious. She's always had a good grip on her emotions.

Renwick actually looks excited. Like, he's actually got a grin on his face.

He always was a loon. Though you'd never guess it from his hulking size and the scruff that's always on his face because he's too lazy to shave his beard more than once every two weeks.

And then there is Davorian. His brows are furrowed, his expression absolutely focused. I can see it in the set of his shoulders and the way he walks. He doesn't want to get his hopes up, because after all these years, after testing so many ultralights before they manifest, we've never found the gatekeeper. But still, what if…?

There is nothing more intimidating than a posse of darkling warriors, the ones tough enough to survive nearly two centuries of being hunted. But Jaxon only stands a little straighter, and never once looks away from them.

"Everyone, this is Jaxon Gray," I say, jumping in before anyone else can say anything and say the wrong thing. "Jaxon, this is Ascelin, Philomena, Renwick, and Davorian." I say their names as I indicate each one.

"I'd say it's nice to meet you, but considering you're going to want to kill us in a few days, seems a little ingenuine," Ascelin says. His tone is hard, but the look in his eyes is harder.

"Ascelin," Davorian immediately chides. "He didn't get to choose this any more than you did."

Ascelin's jaw clenches hard, and the accusations in his eyes don't lighten.

"Killing people has never really been my favorite," Jaxon says, never once looking away from Ascelin. "I'm aiming for that not to change if what Serena says is true."

I look over at him and my eyes narrow.

Never been his favorite? Does that mean he has though?

I mean…look at his family.

I guess I shouldn't be surprised.

Or it's all a front?

I shake my head. It doesn't matter.

"We're glad you both made it back safe," Davorian says. "In just a few minutes this will all be over, and you can go back to your life."

"Hey, don't just dismiss it already," Renwick says, and he genuinely looks bugged that we aren't even considering that this might be it. "It's bound to happen at some point."

No one says anything to that.

"Let's get this over with," Ascelin says, never once looking away from Jaxon, still staring him down like he'll kill him right now if he breathes wrong.

Davorian turns first, walking back down the hall. Ascelin stands where he is, eyeing Jaxon as everyone starts back down the hall, headed for the gate.

"Lighten up," I hiss to him as I walk by, right behind Jaxon. "Why are you acting like this?"

He's always on edge whenever we've tested a new ultralight, but this is different.

"Why are you running off with an ultralight?" he growls.

My eyes narrow at him and something hardens in my stomach.

I've known it for years. And really, I guess I shouldn't be surprised. We've been stranded for so many years, and we're all each other has.

I've noticed the longing look in his eyes in the last decade.

I've noticed how he will stick around longer than necessary.

How he's protested so strongly when I said I needed to get my own place and moved out of living at the compound full-time.

Ascelin has feelings for me.

Or, at least, he thinks he does.

I'm one of only three female options in the immediate vicinity in the LightVerse that is his own kind.

Nisha is cold and detached. Philomena and Renwick have been hooking up since the nineteen-twenties.

So all he's left with is me.

That's not real feelings.

And besides, my heart hasn't been open since the

gate closed. Since sixty years passed, and I knew he was dead.

So, I ignore his question, and I follow behind Jaxon down the hallway.

He's taking it all in as he goes. His head turns left and right as we march him down. He sees the bunk room. A bunch of bedrooms. The door is slightly cracked into the armory, and he gets a good view of just how well stocked we are. He sees offices and the kitchen.

My heart starts racing as we approach the heart of the compound. The space opens into a wide area. There are screens all around. Nisha is there, looking at one of them, the one that shows the zones and all the ultralights.

And there, straight ahead, is the railing.

I don't know if I can handle one more disappointment. I've already given up hope that we will ever return home. But still, it kills another little part of me when each test comes back negative.

The darklings spread out along the railing. I step up to Jaxon's side as we walk up to it, and I watch his expression when it comes into view.

He's nervous. He has every right to be. I can tell he doesn't know what to expect when he sees it. And I doubt that he expected it to be a pit in the ground.

But as his eyes meet it, they grow a little wider. I see the reflection of the surface of it ripple in his eyes.

"You simply touch it," Davorian instructs. "You can kneel at the opening and reach down to it. If you are not the gatekeeper, it will simply feel like smoke, and then solid."

Jaxon's eyes rise up to meet his, and I see the unspoken question there. *And if I am…?*

But he doesn't say anything. He simply takes a step forward.

I look down at the gate. The metal railing circles around it, fully encompassing it except for one section, where the bars turn down and attach to the ground. There are stairs that lead down from it, kind of like a swimming pool.

Beneath that, shadows swirl and there are small ripples of light that dance beneath the surface. Purple, blue, gray.

Home is so close, yet so far away.

I find myself swallowing hard as I watch Jaxon lower onto his knees. My heart is pounding in my throat. Even my hearing feels messed up, adrenaline and fear and hope are surging so hard through my body.

Every single darkling takes a step forward. No one breathes.

Jaxon looks over at me one last time. I can see his plea for help in his eyes. I can see his need for reassurance.

This feels crazy.

He's seeing a swirling, unearthly vortex below him, in a sandstone pit in the middle of the desert.

I hold my breath, and I give him one nod.

So, he looks back down at the gate, and slowly, he reaches down into the depths.

Jaxon's fingers reach for the gate, lowering an inch at a time.

His fingers slip into the smoke.

And I wait for it, for when his hand will hit something solid. For when he knocks on it. When he looks up and asks if there's literally a physical door that's closed beneath the smoke.

But his entire hand slides down into the smoke.

And I watch it as the lights beneath the surface pulse as they flash from purple and blue, to white.

The entire surface of the gate ripples, and brilliant light stirs beneath the surface of the dark smoke.

"No freaking way," Renwick says in a breathy exhalation.

Jaxon looks up, unsure what this means. He meets my eyes, but all I can do is keep staring at the pulsing white light. My throat is tight, my mouth is dry.

"He's the one," Davorian says. He sounds just as breathless. "You are the gatekeeper."

"Took long enough," Philomena says. "We've only been waiting around for you for 158 years."

Jaxon keeps looking at me, waiting for me to say something.

I am his source of explanation, where this all started for him. He's looking for answers, for reassurance, but I find myself rooted, frozen in disbelief.

158 years. It's been 158 years. I never thought we'd get to go back.

What happens next, happens so fast, I hardly even get time to react.

Ascelin grabs Jaxon by his shirt, yanking him back so hard, he rips Jaxon's shirt in half. As Jaxon gives a yell and his fists fly, Ascelin shifts in an instant. Jaxon is enveloped in smoke and shadow, and fangs snap in Jaxon's face as he tries to fight back.

In a skitter of pincers and roils of shadows, Ascelin hauls Jaxon across the space. The door to the vault is opened, and Ascelin throws Jaxon inside.

I shift in an instant and throw myself at Ascelin. I slam into him as he's trying to pull the door closed, knocking him sideways.

Ascelin rolls to the side before clamoring to claws and feet. He lets out an unearthly scream at me, even as I jump on top of him, pinning him to the ground with my claws.

"What do you think you're doing?" I hiss at him, the sound coming out shuddered and sonic. It reverberates off the walls, coming back to my own ears, formed somewhere on my ever-shifting body.

"We can't ever let him go now," Ascelin roars, his

voice demonic and terrifying. "He'll try to run. He'll try to kill us all when he manifests."

"You cannot simply throw him in the vault and let him rot for the rest of his life!" I yell as Ascelin throws me off and skitters back toward Jaxon, who stands in the doorway, breathing hard, his eyes wide. His hands are rolled into fists, as if he could ever fight a darkling.

"Only until the other gatekeeper returns," Ascelin says in a hiss as he reaches out for Jaxon.

Another darkling slams into Ascelin—Renwick. He grips Ascelin and spins, throwing him against one of the sandstone walls. With a hissing howl that rattles sand from the roof above us, Renwick positions himself between Jaxon and Ascelin.

"Enough!" Davorian roars, his human voice barely competing with the darkling screams. "Stand down, Ascelin. We will work through this like human beings, not war lords."

Ascelin climbs to his feet again, staring at Davorian with his glowing, ember eyes.

"Stand. Down." Davorian's voice shudders with anger and command. I see in his eyes the strength of a general. The determination of a darkling.

Ascelin and I stare each other down for another solid thirty seconds. His eyes shift to Jaxon, who still stands in the doorway of the vault, his knees bent, his fists up, and fight in his eyes.

And finally, he shifts back into human form. The look of death in his eyes hasn't diminished one bit.

I walk to Renwick's side, and we both shift back at the same time. But neither of us moves.

What a weird turn this situation has taken. Two darklings protecting an ultralight from one of our own.

"If you need to leave, Ascelin, then leave," Davorian says.

"I think I'll stay," he growls out.

"I will immediately transfer you to the China sector if there is any further issue," Davorian warns, and from the look on his face, I don't doubt him one bit.

Ascelin glares at Davorian for two seconds, and then turns and walks to take a seat next to Nisha.

She hasn't moved a muscle or said a word this entire time.

"You okay?" I ask, looking back at Jaxon.

"I thought you said you all needed me?" he growls. "I only came here with your promise that no one was going to try to kill me."

"I swear, no one else will put you in harm's way again," Davorian says. He takes a step forward, keeping his eyes fixed on Jaxon. "I apologize for Ascelin's behavior. That is not the darkling way."

Jaxon shifts from one foot to the other, and he looks nervous, but ready to fight. I think he's finally realizing the weight of the situation. He's human, for now, and he's surrounded by six darklings. "So, what? I'm just going to be your prisoner for the rest of my life?"

My gaze slips over to Davorian at that, who looks at Nisha, who looks at Renwick, who looks back at me.

"So that's a yes," Jaxon says. His voice is hard.

"It's not like that," Davorian says. He takes another step forward. "I don't know what all Serena has explained to you. But, we do need you until the gatekeeper in the DarkVerse comes to the gate. Only then can it be opened, and we can return home."

"So, what? I just have to sit there with my hand in that hole until they decide to show up?" he asks. His tone is rising, and I can tell he's getting more panicked by the moment that he really is a prisoner here and that I've tricked him.

I never thought I was. Because I never thought he would actually be the gatekeeper.

"The gate reacts on both sides when it is touched by a gatekeeper," Nisha says, speaking for the first time since all this madness began. "When the darkling gatekeeper touches the gate on that side, we can tell here. It ripples. It goes pitch black. Just like you just saw when it reacted to you, only in the dark reverse."

Davorian nods. "So, we will always need you to stay close. But no, you won't be chained to the pit, doomed to sit there forever."

Jaxon's jaw loosens just a little bit with that information, but he's still ready for a fight. "And how long has it been since it last reacted on this side?"

Once more, everyone kind of looks away from each other and the awkward tension in the air doubles.

"Thirty-one years," Philomena answers in a monotone voice.

Jaxon's hard eyes slide over to me. "So yes, I'll be expected to be at your beck and call every moment for the rest of my life."

"It's not like that," I say, jumping to explain myself. "There was a three-year period where it reacted all the time. Daily. The DarkVerse gatekeeper was there, waiting for us. But then it stopped, and it's likely because the gatekeeper on that side died. Sometimes it takes a bit for a new one to be born. Likely, they already have been born. We just have to wait for them to manifest and be brought to the gate."

Why do I feel like I'm lying?

That is the logical explanation.

But…

"But you all have been looking for…a gate-keeper…me, for 158 years," Jaxon points out, his gaze growing darker by the moment. "Why would it be any different on that side?"

"Because the darklings aren't unorganized idiots like the ultralights are," Ascelin hisses. I'm impressed he's kept his mouth shut this long.

Davorian looks over at him and glares his last warning.

"It's true, though," Philomena says. "We're not like the ultralights. They're just a bunch of wanna-be angels running around taking care of the Dusk here and there. The darklings are organized. We all trained at the Academy. We have ranks. We track new manifestations. I have to think, if we're stranded here, there are ultralights stranded there. They'd want to get home just as bad as us. The darklings will be brought to the gate as soon as they are found."

That is, if they do not see it as too dangerous.

The last time the gate was opened, hundreds died, and we broke out into a bloody war.

The only motivation the darklings have in opening the gate again, is in hopes that we will return.

But they also have no reason to think we're still alive, unless they've been interacting with any ultralights on that side. No one would have guessed that we'd be invisible to time in the opposite verse.

And unless ultralights survived on that side, the darklings in the DarkVerse would have no reason to think any of us survived in the LightVerse.

I don't cry. I have never, ever been a crier.

But now, with so much changed, and once more, so much to be uncertain about, I feel emotion stinging the back of my eyes.

"We're asking that you be patient," I say, looking

over at Jaxon. "You're going to manifest in a few days, maybe a week. It can be a confusing, dangerous time. It's not easy controlling it in the beginning, ultralight or darkling. If you stay here, we'll keep you and everyone else safe."

I take a step closer to Jaxon, and I hope and pray to the dark that he can see how much I mean my words. "The Kindred are looking for you. If they find you, you won't have much of a choice but to go with them. They'll train you to hunt and kill us. You won't see your old life, your family, ever again."

I reach forward, and even though everyone is watching me, I take his hand. "If you stay with us, we won't force you to hunt down and kill anyone. And you can still see your family."

Ascelin makes a noise, like he was about to roar out a counter but cuts it off when Davorian shoots him a glare.

My eyes look around to the others. I shouldn't be promising this. It's not fully my promise to make.

But as I look at him, I feel protective of Jaxon. Even though he is absolutely a person who doesn't need protecting.

And I see in his eyes that he trusts me.

There is something between us, and neither of us is able to break it.

"Fine," he says. He looks around at the others, and he doesn't drop my hand right away. "But I don't want to be locked up in some room like I'm a prisoner. You all can watch me, put cameras on me, whatever. Just don't put me in a cage."

Ascelin makes another noise, but holds it in. I can feel the heat growing around him. The surface of his skin shifts and stretches as his darkling form fights to break free. It's taking his last ounce of self-control not to shift and take Jaxon.

"You have our word," Davorian says. He takes a step forward and extends his hand. "If you will help us, we will trust you."

Jaxon studies his hand for a minute. I wonder if he feels like he's making a deal with a demon, down here in the dark, hidden deep in a tunnel in the desert.

But he reaches forward, and he shakes Davorian's hand.

Chapter Nine

"Come on, I'll get you settled in a room," I say.

Jaxon looks back at the others, but I can tell he's relieved to be walking away from their scrutinizing eyes. Together, we walk down the hall.

I'm listening for the activities of the others behind me. Davorian and Nisha go to the coms, getting the word out to all of the other agents across the world that the gatekeeper has been found.

I wonder then, will they all return here? They must, I suppose. Because if the DarkVerse gatekeeper touches the gate, we have to be prepared to go back right away. We can't wait for the other agents to cross the entire world to go through.

With that in mind, I aim for one of the private rooms, furthest from the bunkroom.

It's about to be filled once more.

I turn into it and push the door open. "Here you are," I say.

Jaxon takes it in as he walks inside. It's simple. Really simple. There is a twin sized bed pushed against the farthest wall. A small nightstand next to it. A chair in the corner. And that's it.

"Still feels like a prison cell," Jaxon says as he steps inside. "With no windows."

"Yeah, well, windows aren't our favorite things in this place," I say with an exasperated sigh.

"Can you really see in the dark?" Jaxon asks, stating it as if it just occurred to him.

"Of course," I say. "Everyone in the DarkVerse can. Truth be told, I felt half blind in the LightVerse for the first three years. It took a long time for my eyes to adjust."

Jaxon turns in the room, taking stock of it all. But he turns, resting his hands on his hips. "It just doesn't seem right to me, living in the dark. It's just…unnatural."

I scoff at that. "What about living in the sun is natural? Think about it. The sun is constantly trying to kill us. It burns you. It gives you cancer. It wears your skin into leather. You get heat exhaustion. It even evaporates your water, which you need to survive. So if you're talking about living in an unnatural state, I'd argue it's you guys."

It's a rare thing, so when it happens, my heart does

this little…skip. Jaxon smiles. Not something big. Really, it's just in one corner of his mouth. But it tugs there, revealing his white teeth. "You put it that way, and for some reason you start to make sense."

I smirk and nod. "Get some rest," I say, standing in the doorway. "I'm going to make some lunch. I'll bring you some in a little bit."

He doesn't argue with me. Jaxon just sinks down on the bed and lies back, staring up at the ceiling.

I step out and pull the door closed behind me.

Not that he has much privacy. There's a big window looking into his room.

Ascelin comes walking down the hallway. In his hand, he holds a camera and a screw gun.

"Really?" I ask, fixing him with a glare.

"He said I could put cameras on him, so long as I didn't lock him up," Ascelin shoots back, his tone daring me to argue with him. "I'm not doing anything outside of what he gave me permission to do."

I stand there, my arms folded over my chest, while I watch him install the camera. Jaxon is looking at Ascelin from inside the bedroom. "You don't have to act like a dick, you know. We do actually need him. Life will be a lot easier if we just try to get along. He's being exceptionally calm about all of this, considering everything we're throwing on him. It's not going to help anything if you go and blow everything up."

Ascelin finishes screwing the camera into the ceiling. He takes a second to adjust it, looking in at Jaxon to be sure it's aimed in the right direction.

"And you all seem to have forgotten what they're capable of," Ascelin says as he walks away from the room, back down the hall. "How many of them have killed how many of us."

I step in his way before he can pass me. I raise my shirt, exposing the burn marks still visible in my skin. The cuts and bruises on my face and the rest of my body are nearly gone, but they remain. "Trust me, I haven't forgotten."

Ascelin's nostrils flare and his eyes narrow as he takes in my burned skin.

"He's not like the others, Ascelin," I say as I lower my shirt. "You know how it is, usually there's this clear black and white personality when it comes to ultralights. He's not like that. And all of this explaining? It's been through the mouth of a darkling."

I can see that he doesn't want to listen to me. That he doesn't want to see any kind of reason.

"He could change things," I say. My tone sounds a little desperate. "He could mend things between the ultralights and the darklings. I mean, he could even end the Kindred, somehow…"

"And why would he ever be motivated to do that?" Ascelin asks, his tone hard. "You remember the instincts, Serena. How do you ever expect him to fight it? How can you ever hope that he'll overcome that, and then want to help us?"

I shouldn't hope for any of that. I shouldn't expect it. Because I know that likely Ascelin is going to be right. More than likely.

It's pretty much a guarantee.

But still, I hope.

Without another word, Ascelin stalks past me, back to do whatever he's doing.

Probably installing ten times as many cameras.

I ignore him, and head into the kitchen.

I'm the only one of the darklings who doesn't live here full time, so the kitchen is fully stocked. I open the fridge and pull out the makings for sandwiches.

"Look at you, bringing in the gatekeeper." I don't even glance over my shoulder when I hear Renwick walk in. I simply shrug. "Gotta say, Serena, I was starting to doubt you when it took you so long to get the gatekeeper in here. But then Philomena and I tracked that Kindred down, and now I'm kind of impressed you held your own against him, one on one. *While* keeping him away from the gatekeeper. He was a nasty bugger."

"The *gatekeeper* has a name," I say. I don't know what's wrong with me. I feel so snappy. I feel angry and sharp. These are my people, my family. And ever since I came back, I'm so on edge I'm afraid of what I'm going to do or say. "Jaxon. He's not just some tool. He's still a person."

I finish building our sandwiches and finally turn to face Renwick.

He's studying my face, trying to read what's really going on. "He's not what you expected, I get that," he says. "Just don't forget where this ends. With us going home, and him staying here."

He turns, and walks out of the kitchen, leaving me alone with my thick throat.

I snatch the sandwiches from the counter and dig out a few packs of chips from a cupboard. I stalk back down the hallway and let myself back into Jaxon's room. He was still lying on the bed, staring up at the ceiling. I don't want to keep looking at him, don't want to keep reading his every emotion. I'm constantly looking into his eyes trying to decipher what he's feeling. And it's starting to drive me a little crazy.

So I set his sandwich and the chips on the night-stand next to him and I turn and walk straight out of the bedroom. I close the door behind me.

I'm really not very subtle. I put Jaxon in the room right next to mine. I haven't spent more than a night or two in this bedroom in at least three years. But there's no way that I can risk going back to my apartment in the city. Not with Ascelin acting like he's going to murder Jaxon at every turn.

I need a break from Jaxon right now. I need space to clear my head.

I go to my closet and survey my options. There are a few pairs of pants here, a few shirts as well, everything black. I go to the cupboard that holds all my things and rummage through the drawers. I have everything I need here, all of the basics. Everything is a little dusty but it's ready to go.

I wolf down my sandwich, realizing how hungry I am. With all of the insanity going on in the last few days I'm pretty sure I've only eaten two whole meals.

When I'm finished eating, I grab a set of clean clothes and head down to the washroom. It's a large open space. Sort of like the bathroom you would find at the gym. There's a row of toilet stalls, and another row of shower stalls. There's a common area for sinks and a row of mirrors above them. I head into the last shower stall and turn the water on straight cold.

The dark is comforting here. When we are above the surface I feel as if we're in a constant battle with the sun. It's exhausting. It drains me faster than just about any fight ever did.

Here in the dark, in the cold, I miss home more than anything.

I miss brisk nights. I miss walking down the streets with crowds of people around me, all enjoying the comfort of the night sky. I miss looking up into the sky and seeing just stars and the moon. I miss sleeping with thick curtains blocking out the sunlight during the day. I miss the north, where in the winter, the days are so exceptionally long. I miss hibernating during the summer, when the days are long.

I miss my people, things felt… Normal… Natural.

But it's been so long now, it's hard to even comprehend the possibility that I could be returning to it soon. Maybe it will be in two months. Maybe it will be in four years. Maybe it's going to be in fifteen years. But at this point, after one hundred and fifty-eight years, anything would be soon.

I finish up my shower and get dressed. I comb through my unruly hair, and, just to make myself feel better, I dab on a small bit of makeup. I toss my dirty clothes into a hamper.

Now that I'm back, I'll be put back on the chore rotation. It's just like living in any other family. Everyone has to pull their own weight.

I walk out of the bathroom and turn down the hall to return to the command center.

Nisha is busy at the control panels. I can hear her on the phone, quickly talking to another agent on the other end. Davorian is seated beside her and he's on the phone as well. But the second he sees me he looks up and quickly gets off the line.

"I'm ready for debriefing," I say as he walks over to me. He simply gives a nod and the two of us head to one of the conference rooms.

I go over everything with him. I tell him about Jaxon's crime family. I tell him about following him that night and seeing his brother AJ get shot. I tell him about the doctor who tried to save his brother. I tell him about the funeral, how quickly it happened, and then I get to the point where he got in the car with me and pointed a gun in my face, demanding to know who I was, and why I was following him.

I go over my fight with the ultralight in as much detail as I can. Davorian asks questions about who might've seen our fight. And I tried to think through it, if there was any possibility that anyone had seen us.

Of course, there was always a possibility. In just about any other town, the vast majority of people would have been asleep. But this is Las Vegas. There will be traffic jams in the middle of the night, people heading home at four a.m. after a long night of gambling. I didn't see anyone around us that night, but there's always the slim chance that somebody was looking out the window at just the right time.

I then recount how we stole a car and hit the road. I tell Davorian about the first hotel that we stayed in and how Jaxon didn't run, even though he definitely should have. I tell him about the hotel we stayed at in St. George, our stop at the store getting supplies. I share every detail that I can think of leading up to when we returned here to the compound.

However, I do not tell him about the club. I do not

tell him that our time together then was one of the major reasons why Jaxon didn't run. I do not tell him about the stolen glances between the two of us. I do not tell him about the odd trust that we've found in each other.

I do not tell him about the complex emotions that are gripping my chest.

"And now we wait," Davorian says as he leans back in his chair. He crosses one ankle over the opposite one. All this time, all this fighting, all these wars, and he can still find calm in the most uncertain moments. "He showed up on our radar on Sunday. It's Tuesday. Not that we often stick around for this part, but it seems typical that the ultralights manifest within seven to fourteen days once they show up on our radar. Seems we have a bit to prepare for him to manifest."

"Not gonna lie, I'm a little bit worried about that part," I say. I don't look him in the eye. Instead, I trace patterns on the table with my finger. "I've only seen it happen twice. Every time they've manifested, they just exploded into sonic light. I think we're going to have no choice but to lock him in the vault when it happens."

He understood why this was problematic. It was Jaxon's one specific request.

"He seems to trust you for some reason," Davorian says. "Sounds like you need to have a talk with him. I think he'll listen to you."

I nod. I'm planning on it, I'm just not looking forward to the part where I tell him that we do indeed have to actually lock him up.

"How much have you explained to him?" Davorian asks.

"I've told him about the DarkVerse, explained the LightVerse. He's seen me in my darkling form, and now he's seen that I'm not the only one who can do it. And he was fully present when the Kindred attacked. So, he has seen what he's going to become. I explained the gate keeper, and how there's one on each side. I briefly explained the dusk, but I don't think he has any kind of grasp on what that actually means. But I haven't gotten to the war yet."

"It's a lot to explain," Davorian says. "You seem to have done a good job of it given the amount of time you've had. As you said, he is surprisingly calm about all of this."

I nod my head, but I don't say anything about that because I think the main reason for it is that odd, inexplicable connection between the two of us.

"What are you going to do about Ascelin?" I ask. "He can't continue on like this. He can't keep being so possessive. He has no right, and it's going to cause us problems."

"Matters of the heart always complicate things," Davorian says. There's weight that enters his voice and I know he's thinking about his wife he left behind when he left for war. There's no doubt that she's been dead for over a century. "Ascelin's lonely. We're all lonely. But you are right, he has to stop. If you don't reciprocate his feelings, he has to accept that."

And maybe this was part of the problem. I have never made it explicitly clear that I'm not interested. I'm not. I don't have feelings for him like that. Ascelin is more like a brother. After all these years fighting together, nothing has changed for me. If feelings haven't started to develop for him by this point, they never will.

I have to talk to him. I have to make it exceptionally clear.

"I'll deal with this," I say around a thick throat. I have never been one to avoid confrontation, but this is something different. I don't want to go breaking any hearts, even if they have been misplaced.

"We are all relying on you, Serena," Davorian said. I could feel his eyes studying me. "You're taking the lead on this. So, thank you for everything you're doing."

I simply nod. I have nothing else to say, so I stand from my chair and push it back under the table. I walk out without another word.

# Chapter Ten

"I NEED A CELL PHONE."

I look up from where I'm sitting on my bed. We all slept uneasy last night, so we're all being lazy today. It's evening now, and I've done nearly nothing all day.

Jaxon stands in my doorway, one hand tucked into his front pocket.

"My family is going to get suspicious again if they don't hear from me soon," he says as he leans one shoulder against the door frame. "Now, I don't anticipate them being able to track me down to here. But things will be a lot easier and smoother if I can give them some kind of cover story."

I get up from the bed and cross to the door. "Come with me," I say as I step around him.

We walk down the hallway and I push the door open to the armory. I step inside and cross to a cupboard that's in the corner. I pull it open and rummage through a drawer. There, I find an entire stash of burner phones. I pull one out and hand it over to him. "There you go."

Jaxon looks up at me with a peculiar look. "You all don't exactly operate above board here, do you?"

"I guess we have that in common," I answer with a little bit of snark in my voice. "Though our reasons for operation are just a little bit different."

"What, you're not running around taking fingers when people can't pay their debts?" Jaxon asks with that little bit of a smirk in the corner of his mouth.

I give a small smile as well. "It might have something to do with the fact that we've been in this area for a century and a half, yet none of us has aged a single day."

We turn and I find myself wandering down to the heart of the compound. I pull up a chair alongside the gate and sink down into it. Jaxon sits along the wall, plopping right down on the floor.

"You haven't explained that part yet," he says. "How the darklings even got stuck on this side in the first place."

"It's a story of mystery, and…murder."

We both turn to see Renwick walking up. He's got his classic smirk on his face. He walks over and pulls out one of the office chairs from the conference room. He spins it around and sits on it backwards.

Jaxon smirks at Renwick, and I hope, just for a second, that all these olive branches Renwick is extending to Jaxon are the start of a peaceful relationship between the darklings and this ultralight.

"He's kind of right," I say, diving into the history. "And parts of it…they seem almost impossible."

"I've watched you transform into a shadow spider monster multiple times now," Jaxon says as he raises an eyebrow. "I don't know that anything sounds impossible now."

I chuckle, looking down at my hands in my lap. I take a deep breath and look down at the gate. "Okay, well, the Dusk has always been around, so that means the darklings and the ultralights have always been around." Jaxon nods, and I'm glad he's keeping up. "This is the part that seems too impossible to me. That an ultralight and a darkling were at the gate at the same time. Look at this place. It's in an underground *tunnel*. And back then, too. I mean, Las Vegas in the DarkVerse is *nothing*." I shake my head, thinking of just how nothing it is. "It's too sunny here, too hot. So, the fact that a darkling was even there was a huge coincidence. But they were both here, at the same time. And by some miracle, they both touched the gate at the same time."

"And it opened," Jaxon states.

I nod.

"As the stories are told, they both just…marveled at

each other for a moment. I can only imagine how impossible it was to comprehend. But they started asking questions. They started realizing that their worlds were mirrors of one another, but opposites. The light and the dark."

"It blew my mind, the first time I learned about the LightVerse," Renwick says. "The idea that there were people out there who lived their lives during the daytime…" He shook his head.

"And that was before people even knew about the doppelganger part," I say, raising an eyebrow. "That's the part that really got me."

"Still not so sure I believe you on that part," Jaxon says, and from the look in his eyes, I can tell he means that.

"Anyway," I say, choosing to move on, "the gate was discovered a month after I manifested."

"A year after I did," Renwick adds to the details.

"The gatekeeper didn't get word to us at the academy at first," I say. "There were telegrams by that point, but for obvious reasons, we couldn't use them. And how could that be explained in a short message."

"Was it the same as it was here?" Jaxon asks. "I mean, the mid-eighteen hundreds, there would have been, what, the Pony Express?"

"It went bankrupt a few years before this," I say. I lived through this part of history, and it feels as far back as it was. "Telegrams were so much more cost effective. And you have to remember, Nevada hadn't even become a state quite then, and we were in the middle of the American Civil War still. But yes, it was the same there as it is here. Don't forget, the same people here are the same people we have back there. We still had George Washington and Alexander Hamilton, Abraham Lincoln—though they had different names in the DarkVerse."

It's kind of beautiful, really. The symmetry between the light and the dark.

"The gatekeepers came to an agreement. They would return with their fellow guardians, the ultra-lights and the darklings, and show each other what had been found. They would both be gone for the span of four months. That's how long it would take to get back to the darkling academy and then return again."

"Where is the academy?" Jaxon asks, his brows furrowing.

"Upstate New York," I answer. "Though the commanders were talking about finding a new location, further west, because of how populated the east coast was becoming. We had a job to do in tracking down and excising the Dusk, but we needed our space, somewhere safe to train the darklings."

"So, what she's saying, is there's no chance the academy is still in New York, and if we get to go home, we won't even know where to look for them all,"

Renwick says the words we've all dreaded for more than a century.

The silence is heavy for a moment. It's a lot to think over. I've run through the possibilities in my head so many times. It would still be in the north, but would they have even stayed in the States? It could easily be in Canada. Or they could have gone farther. One of the darkest places in the world is in Norway, because of the mountains, where there's almost no sunlight at all for six months out of the year. The most northern part of Alaska can go two whole months without sun. Though that's countered by three months straight of the sun always being in the sky. And then there are the Faroe Islands, which only receive about thirty-seven days of sunshine a year.

That sounds like heaven.

If only it weren't quite so cold there.

"Anyway," I continue on. "The darkling gatekeeper returned to New York and told the commanders what she had learned and seen. So, a group of six hundred and fifty of us headed southwest to see the unbe-lievable."

Jaxon looks up at me, and I know what he's likely thinking. That it seems impossible that I could have been there, back in the eighteen-hundreds, that I was literally a part of this history.

"I was the newest at the academy," I say. "I'd only manifested three and a half months earlier."

"But you'd never have known it," Renwick says with a smile as he looks at me. "She was so angry it made her one of the deadliest darklings the academy had ever seen."

"Why doesn't that surprise me?" Jaxon goads.

A small smile pulls in the corner of my mouth, and I just shake my head.

"It was such a long journey," I said. "A caravan of that size doesn't move fast, even though there was a train to take us a third of the way. And we had to take food, water, weapons with us. We would travel as darklings during the day, so as not to be seen, but the light was brutal, and the heat was nearly enough to kill us. This was the dead of summer."

Renwick shakes his head, and I remember how hard the heat had been for him to handle. He had always been a huge guy. He'd guzzled more water than any of us.

"We arrived in the desert and Davorian ordered us to set up camp, a mile out from the gate. He didn't want to overwhelm the ultralights and cause a problem. We'd brought an entire army, after all. He wanted peace, no matter what. So he, and the gatekeeper, and a few others went to the gate that night."

"They talked," Renwick continues. "And they each crossed over into the other's verse. Davorian and the others agreed that they would continue to talk, share what they knew about each other's verses."

"But during the day, the ultralight gatekeeper opened the gate. The darkling gatekeeper was sleeping, right at the gate, so they were able to open it up. A dozen ultralights snuck through, and explored our verse, even though they weren't supposed to do it without being accompanied by our gatekeeper and Davorian."

"Davorian hadn't told the ultralights that he'd come with an army," Renwick says. "So, when they snuck through, it didn't take them long before they found our camp."

"They were probably scared," I say, looking from him to Jaxon. "I would have been too if someone I didn't know had brought an entire army and didn't tell me about it. The ultralights ran back to the gate, went through, and closed it."

My gaze is hazy, and I'm not really seeing the floor of the compound. I'm seeing outside, the desert in the DarkVerse. "We waited for a week for the gate to open again. Our gatekeeper stayed there the entire time. Davorian got the report that someone had seen ultralights scouting out the camp. We didn't know what to expect."

"And one morning, on the hottest and brightest damn day of the year, they came back through with their own army," Renwick says with a hard voice.

"I thought you said the ultralights aren't very organized and don't know anything about war?" Jaxon asks.

Renwick shakes his head. "Not anymore. But back then, it was different. Back then, they had Hyrum Ashmore."

Jaxon's brows furrow at just the name alone and he looks over at me.

"He was the ultralight version of Ascelin," I say. And as the words leave my lips, my stomach goes cold.

That gets Jaxon's attention.

I look down the hall, making sure that Ascelin isn't within hearing distance. "He was legendary," I admit. "The darklings are exceptional fighters. We all train. But none of us were like Hyrum. He commanded the ultralights and none of them questioned a single order. And I had never, and have never since, seen anyone who fought like Hyrum. Except for Ascelin."

"No wonder he's such a tool," Jaxon says, his gaze turning dark as he recalls every horrible interaction in the past twenty-four hours.

The truth is, Ascelin is as hard as he is in part because of Hyrum Ashmore. He's seen a shadow of what he could have become. The glorified commander. The legend.

Instead, Ascelin chose a different path. He's always been the best of us when it came to fighting. But he chose to teach at the academy, instead of seeking out glory and commander positions.

"The ultralights thought we were preparing to attack them," Renwick moves on. "And maybe we would have, if we'd thought there was a threat. We were simply being prepared. But they took our presence as a declaration. The war exploded instantly."

War is one of those words that gets a reaction out of anyone. They grow quiet. You see their shoulders drop. There's a certain look in their eyes.

I feel it in me. I see it on Jaxon.

"It lasted three weeks," I say, the words coming out quiet and hoarse. "It flowed from one side to the other. Dozens were killed on the first day. Fifty the next. There was no talking. No reason or explanation was made. It was just bloody and grew in intensity with every crossing between verses."

"You said my natural instinct is going to be to kill you," Jaxon said. "Both sides, they couldn't help it, could they?"

My eyes slide to Jaxon. I shake my head.

I remember the feeling. Every time an ultralight came into our verse, it was as if the shadows inside of me surged and the monster in me could only think to eliminate them.

"After twenty-one bloody days, a huge surge of darklings overtook the gate and forced our way into the LightVerse," I continue. "We were winning. Many of the ultralights were retreating. But it happened so suddenly."

"One of our darklings accidentally killed the Light-Verse gatekeeper," Renwick tells the part that dammed us to our desertion here.

"The gate instantly closed. The ultralights retreated. Hyrum was killed during the battle that day. And so we turned to leave, to go home. And that's when we found the gatekeeper lying there, dead. And the gate was closed."

"We didn't really understand it yet," Renwick says. His voice is hoarse as well, and I know this is just as hard for him to tell the story as it is for me. "We all touched the gate, over and over. Every single one of us, trying to open the gate. But it didn't respond."

"And then we knew," I say. "We understood. And we realized that we were stuck in the LightVerse."

There are so many more details that I could go in to. How we nearly died in the first few weeks from starvation and dehydration. How we all started to go a little mad. And then how we had to build shelter.

"We had to keep control of the gate," I continue. "We needed to go home as soon as possible. We just had no idea how impossible it was going to be to find the gatekeeper."

"It involved a lot of kidnapping and a lot of us dying trying to get them back to the gate," Renwick says. "Our numbers dropped quick those first few decades."

I nod. "It was a miracle when we came up with the

tech that can detect a new ultralight, before they manifest."

"What about the Kindred?" Jaxon asks. "The ones who are hunting you down. When did that start?"

"As soon as we started spreading throughout the world," Renwick answers. "I mean, those ultralights that were left when the gate closed tried with everything they had to kill us all off. But we got to most of them before they could do too much damage to our numbers. There would always be someone or even a small group who would come and try to kill us."

"But as time went on, fewer and fewer ultralights even knew about us. So, it was less of a threat. But the Kindred, they knew, and they passed the information down as they found other ultralights to take into their fold. There aren't a ton of them out there, but we always have to be careful."

Jaxon rubbed at his eyes. "I can't… It's just so much. And it still sounds absolutely insane. I wish there was some kind of proof, something I could see now that would tell me I'm the ultralight you say I am. It just seems too impossible to believe."

An idea sparks in my brain. "Come on," I say as I stand. I reach a hand down to him and pull him to his feet.

We don't go far. Just across the command center to the five screens that are all lined up together.

It's the map of the world, and on it, there are thousands of glowing white dots.

"They're all ultralights, all of them around the world," I say. Looking at it, I feel overwhelmed, and a little bit scared. There are so, so many. There are only fifty of us left in this world. And it makes my heart ache, because if there are this many ultralights in the LightVerse, there are this many darklings in the Dark-Verse. "The brighter they are, the newer they are. They glow brightest just before they manifest."

I tap the screen, zooming in on the United States. I tap again, and we drop in on the southwest corner of it. I zoom in even further, highlighting only Nevada.

There are a dozen or so glowing dots in the state. And there are three, right here in Las Vegas.

I zoom in even more, and the three dots' locations become much more accurate.

"Guess which one is you?" I ask, looking over at him.

Jaxon's eyes fix on the one dot, right where we are in the desert. I realize my mistake right then, that I've shown him our exact location. But really, the circumstances have changed. Jaxon is tied to us now, for life.

His dot is glowing twice as bright as the other two.

He doesn't say anything at first, just studies the map.

"There are two other ultralights in Las Vegas?" he asks.

I nod. "They live here. Came in about three years ago. We've been keeping an eye on them, and keeping out of their way. They actually seem like decent people."

"Well, if the ultralights manifest in anyone, wouldn't there be a pretty good chance all of them will be good people?" he asks.

"Actually, yes," I say. "Darkling or ultralight, they're almost always good people. They're loyal and strong. It's part of the evolutionary reason why we exist. There are certain traits needed to do what we do." My eyes slide down to the floor for a moment before looking up at Jaxon. "To be honest, I was kind of shocked when I found out more about you, that you're an ultralight."

Jaxon just looks back at the map without saying anything. And that tells me that he's a little surprised himself, knowing what the general qualifications are.

But I get it now. Now that I've spent time with him.

Jaxon has his dark side. But he didn't get much choice in its formation. Those were simply the circumstances he was born into.

But he's strong. That's obvious by the fact that he's not freaking out.

He's loyal. Even though they're not on the straight and narrow, I can tell how loyal he is to his family.

He's certainly unconventional, but I understand how he came to be the LightVerse's newest ultralight.

## Chapter Eleven

THE NEXT DAY is spent in tense anticipation.

I'm not exactly sure what I'm anticipating. For Ascelin to do something crazy? For Jaxon to finally have the freak out I'm expecting? For a Kindred to burst in here and kill us all in an attempt to take the gatekeeper?

I can't relax the entire next day.

Thankfully, it's spent in meetings. Sort of. Davorian calls us into the command room. Jaxon sticks to himself in his room, entirely unsure of his place, as are we. We talk about what to do from here. Jaxon will have to stay here, in the compound. We don't want to make him our prisoner, but really, how can we ever trust that he won't run?

I worry my lip raw over that one.

My gut tells me he won't run. But my brain says

there's no reason he wouldn't try if given the opportunity. What ultralight wants to spend the rest of their life in the dark, underground, just waiting for the gate to ripple? He could never be that selfless, doing this huge favor and giving up his life to get us home.

Thankfully, it seems the rest of the compound is split on the decision as well. Ascelin, Nisha, and Philomena vote that we can't let him ever leave the compound again. Davorian, Renwick, and I think it's unfair to expect this of him.

But it's a decision for later.

For now, we work on what this change means for us immediately.

The biggest thing is that we no longer need agents out in the field. We're weaker spread out like this, and it only gives the Kindred more opportunities to pick us off, and any other ultralight that does their job.

They're to come home.

The meeting ends that night with Davorian and Nisha sending out the word that the gatekeeper has been found and they're to return to the compound.

It's late when we step out of the command room. I can feel it in my bones, in my mind. I'm on a diurnal schedule now.

I walk down the hall, with my heart beating a little faster.

I peek around the window into Jaxon's room.

He's lying on his bed with his back turned to me.

The blanket is pulled up to his neck and his breaths are slow and even.

"You need to be careful, little spider," Philomena says.

I turn to see her walking up behind me. "What do you mean?"

She raises an eyebrow at me. She stops further down the hall and I walk back to stand across from her. I don't want to wake Jaxon up.

She crosses her arms over her chest and leans back against the wall. "Don't play dumb with me, Serena. You left here three years ago because you were giving up on ever going home. You started to carve out your own version of normal. And then you come back here, with him, and there's something alive in your eyes again."

I just stare at her. I don't like the words that are coming out of her mouth. But I can't argue with them.

"He feels normal to you," Philomena says. Her eyes are screaming a warning to me, but there's also something in them that shows something close to understanding. "He feels like a shadow in the never-ending light we've been stuck in."

Her analogy is ridiculous, considering we're in the LightVerse and Jaxon is an ultralight, but I get what she's saying.

"Just be careful," she says. She pushes off from the

wall and heads toward the room she and Renwick sometimes share. "Ultralights always burn shadows."

My throat is thick, dry, and stuck so that I can't say a word when she steps into the room and closes the door behind her.

I look back at Jaxon's door, and I find myself glaring. I find my stomach twisting.

Why did things have to be this way? Why did it have to be him?

I walk back into my own room and close the door. And I stare up at the ceiling for the next several hours.

THE NEXT MORNING IS CHAOTIC.

Davorian and Nisha are busy getting the other agents to return home. It's not a small, quick job, they've been living lives in their parts of the world now for over a hundred years. They can't instantly pull up roots and leave.

Philomena and Renwick head to the Strip. The three of us field agents have gotten exceptionally good at the tables over the years. We're going to need some extra cash for the influx of people we're about to experience.

Ascelin is installing another wave of security cameras.

I'm just cleaning up from lunch when Jaxon walks

into the kitchen. He leans against the doorway, his arms folded over his chest.

"You still hungry?" I ask. "There's some stuff in the snack cupboard there." I point to it with the butter knife in my hand.

"I'm not hungry," Jaxon says.

I put the last of the dishes in the dishwasher and turn to face him, leaning back against the counter. "You need something else?"

He stares at me for a moment, not saying a thing, and I wonder what's going through his head. I'm noticing this about him, that he's quieter than I expect him to be. He thinks about what he says and does before he does them. And even then, he doesn't always say what's going through his mind.

"What's the decision?" he finally asks. "Am I prisoner here?"

My chest tightens, because I know why he's asking. None of us have hardly spoken a word to him in the past forty-eight hours. But he's seen us meeting, having serious talks. Of course he can tell we're discussing his future.

"No," I say. And I mean it. Somehow, I will make sure that he is not just a prisoner. "It's a complicated situation. I think you get why. But I swear, I won't let you just become a prisoner."

He stares once more, for a heavy moment. "Why?" he asks. He waits another four beats, and I feel everything building. "Why did this have to be us, you and me? Why did we have to be what we are?"

I'm pretty sure my heart falls out of its place in my chest and tumbles down into the bottom of my stomach.

There. He's said what I've been thinking and feeling since the moment he walked out of that casino into the parking garage.

Why him?

I shake my head. "I don't know. It doesn't exactly seem fair, does it?"

"No," Jaxon says. He shakes his head too, just once. He lets out a hard breath and relaxes deeper into the wall he's leaning against. "It's been three years since I've felt anything or even taken a second glance. I…" He trails off, breathing a little hard after blurting out so many words.

"What happened to her?" I ask. Because every-thing in my gut, and his body language, tells me she was there in the past.

Jaxon's eyes rise up from beneath his long lashes to meet mine. He looks at me again, once more thinking about what he says before he says it. He walks into the kitchen and sits on the counter, just two feet away from me.

"Her name was Carley," he says as he fixes his gaze on the tile floor. "We had been together since we were seventeen, since right before Mom made me drop out of high school to start working for her."

There's a lot, right there in that one sentence. It tells me so much more about Jaxon.

"How old are you, by the way?" I ask. "I just realized I have no idea."

He looks over at me for a moment. "I turned twenty-five this last January."

I nod. I'm forever frozen at twenty-two until I can return home. So, physically, he's three years older than me. Even though I'm actually more than a century and a half older than him.

"So, we were together for three years," he continues. His eyes return to the floor. "She was sweet and kind. Came from a good family. Her parents hated me. They really had no idea what my family was like, but I guess you can just tell. It just kind of comes off of me, that I'm not someone who's ever seen what the straight and narrow path looks like."

I can hear the self-hatred in his voice. How much he hates his life, and that he's never really had a choice in it.

My heart aches for him.

We should all have a choice in how we live our lives.

"But Carley never made me feel like I was less than. Like I was a criminal, even when I started working for Mom full-time. She'd just smile and take me out for ice cream, or out to the desert to lie under the stars."

I can see it in his eyes, hear it in the way he speaks. He loved her. He really did.

"I thought I was going to marry her someday," he says. "Or, at least I dreamed about it. I knew she was too good for my world, so I knew I couldn't ever really tie her to me permanently like that. And her parents never would have given their blessing, and she wouldn't have done it without their permission. But we were happy, for those few years."

He looks up, his gaze fixing on the wall across from him. "Three years ago, my family got mixed up in this dirty money war with another loan shark family. It got pretty bad for a while. Blake nearly died. I'm pretty positive Aaron killed their oldest son. I got shot twice when they drove by." His hand comes up to his side, and I'm sure if I could, I'd be seeing two scars. "And then they kidnapped Carley."

All of my insides go cold.

"She was headed to her car after class," he says, and I can hear the strain in his voice. "She was a student at UNLV. They took her back to their house, and an hour later, they sent me and Mom this video of her."

No matter which verse I'm in, there is always evil.

"They'd roughed her up. She was bleeding and crying," he says, his voice shaking. "They said if we didn't back off that they'd torture her for every day the war carried on. If it wasn't over in five days, they'd kill her."

I can't even imagine it. How he must have felt. How scared they both must have been.

"I tried to call it," Jaxon says. "I reached out to every contact I could, but they all told me the same thing. That Mom said it wasn't over. That we couldn't give in to them or we'd never recover. The Grays win, always. So, we planned a siege that night."

Jaxon looks down at his hand, and I notice it's covered with an array of scars. "Blake, Aaron, Griff, and even Chantel stormed their building. It was a shoot first, don't ask questions later kind of situation." He shakes his head. "I'd sworn to myself that I'd never kill anyone for my mother. But that night, I shot Carley's kidnapper right between the eyes."

So this is what he meant, when he'd alluded to killing people.

He's quiet for a moment, and I don't press him. He's living the worst day of his life behind that gaze. I haven't seen much of the Gray family, but I got a small glimpse that day I followed Jaxon.

"I got Carley out of there. She had some bruises and cuts, but other than that, she was okay," he says. His voice is quiet, rough. "But she couldn't look me in the eye. And I just kept telling her how sorry I was, over and over. But I knew it. It was over. I could never put her in danger again. I had to get out of her life before I got her killed. And she couldn't even look at me."

I hear him swallow, like it's the most difficult thing in the world to do. "I took her home to her parents' house and I made her a promise. That I would never see her again, and that she would never be hurt by me and my family again. She didn't argue. She didn't say anything at all when she climbed out of the car and walked to the door."

My insides feel cold. This isn't even my story, but my joints feel stiff with grief, my head feels heavy with guilt.

"She moved to northern Utah just a few weeks later," Jaxon says. "I never contacted her, but I just wanted to make sure she was safe. She's married now. They just had their first baby a few months ago."

He actually sounds happy about this. Like he's happy she got out, that she was able to move past the trauma he caused her. And I just think, *good for her,* as well.

"Ever since then, I've never dared even look at a woman," he says, lifting his chin. "I swore I'd never put anyone else in danger because of my family. My world is too dark, too cut-throat, and as long as my mother lives, there will never be peace in my family."

Jaxon's eyes shift over to me. His lips are loose, as if

words are on the tip of his tongue. His eyes slide down me slowly, and then just as slowly rise back up.

"That night we met at the club," he says. His voice is low, husky. It sends a wave of goosebumps across my skin. "I never thought I'd do that again. I never thought I'd give another woman a second glance. But when you looked at that dick the way you did, like you really were going to kill him if he didn't back down, it just felt…different. You weren't fragile. I could tell you were dangerous. And I just…"

Got drawn in.

I understand.

It was the same way I felt. And it was a cruel twist of fate, that we were both what we are.

"I was engaged," I say. The words leave my lips before I fully give them permission. But I don't regret that they're out now. It's been so long since I've talked about this. "His name was Keir. He was a printer's apprentice. We met in Ohio, before I manifested."

I think back to that time. Things were so much more simple. Yes, people often died of disease and hunger. But we weren't in such a rush, not like now. There was no internet, no mass of devices connecting us. It was…easier.

"He asked me to marry him two weeks before it happened," I say. "My parents loved him, they were happy he was a tradesman, that I wouldn't have to be a farmer's wife. My mother started making my wedding dress the day after I said yes."

My emotions are complicated right now. I loved him. I loved my life.

But it was so, so long ago now. It almost feels more like a dream I had once, not the actual life I lived.

"But one night as I woke up, I felt this…stirring inside of me. I felt less solid. And then it just happened. Thankfully, I was home alone. Mother and Father had already gone into town. But I destroyed half the house as I tried to gain control of this…beast that had taken me over. Don't get me wrong, it was terrifying and confusing. But I felt…incredible."

I shake my head and close my eyes, recalling that first shift. I'd never felt so powerful. It felt so natural. I felt free and wild and amazing.

"Once I was outside, this urge took me over," I say. "It's almost like I could smell it, and once I'd latched onto it, I couldn't focus on anything else. I could sense a Dusk in town. I went straight for it. It was this woman. She had once been a loving mother, but suddenly she was doing all of these crazy things, hurting all of these people.

"I didn't even know what I was doing. I found her in an alley. And I just…knew. I reached inside of her chest with my claws. And I felt it, clean and simple. I pulled it from her, and I knew exactly how to destroy it, to crush it. And the woman, she just collapsed, unconscious. So I took my moment, and I ran."

It had all been such a destructive mess. I probably exposed myself, it's hard to imagine that no one saw me.

"I had to tell my parents," I say. "There was no way to hide it. They came home and the house was half destroyed. And Keir was with them. They didn't believe me. They couldn't understand. So I had to show them. I shifted, and they'd screamed. They screamed so much. They thought I was a demon. They thought I needed to be exorcised."

My lower stomach quivers with the fear and shame I had felt that day.

"But then Davorian showed up," I say, lifting my head. "He senses them, the other darklings that are about to manifest, just like the Kindred. He'd spent the last four days trying to hurry to me, traveling from New York to Ohio. He didn't make it in time to explain what was about to happen, but he got there to keep my parents and me from losing our minds."

It was so strange, the first time I saw him. He walked up the road, and I'd seen him immediately. And something in me just…calmed. It was as if I knew him, had known him my entire life. And I trusted him. I was so relieved to see him, and I didn't even know who he was.

"He explained what I was, why I existed. He told

me, and my parents, and Kier everything that had just happened and what was going to happen. And he told me about the academy. Where all the other darklings were trained. There really wasn't a choice, I had to go and be trained, but he didn't make it seem that way. I was relieved.

"He stayed at the house that day, giving me just one day to settle my life," I say. "My parents couldn't understand. But they couldn't deny what they'd seen me do. But Keir was so quiet. He said almost nothing."

His silence was crippling. It twisted my guts. Made me doubt everything in the entire world.

"When nightfall came, I forced him into a room. I told him I had to know if he still loved me. If he still wanted to be with me, even if I was this creature we had never heard of."

My voice is hoarse. "He told me that he didn't know. That this was too wild, too new. He didn't know how he felt. It crushed me. But I was determined that this would not be the end. That this wouldn't be out of my control. So I struck a deal with him. I would go to the academy, and in three months' time, after he'd had enough time to think about how he felt, he would come to New York, and we would talk then. We would make a decision then."

I look over at Jaxon. His expression is full of sympathy and understanding.

Neither of us has a very good story.

"Two days before Keir was supposed to arrive in New York, we were deployed to the gate," I say. "It wasn't a choice. It wasn't an option. We all had to go, and we had to leave right then. We packed our gear and we left. There was no time to leave a note, no time to explain."

I swallow once. "I never imagined we wouldn't be coming back. I knew that Keir would be upset and hurt that I wasn't there when he'd traveled all that way to talk to me. But I still thought we would get the chance to talk. That I would be back. But…" I shake my head. "But everything with the gate happened. And then we were stuck here."

I fold my arms over my stomach. "So I never knew," I conclude. "I never knew what Keir's decision was going to be. If he was too scared to stay with me. If he thought he could deal with me being a darkling guardian of the verse. I spent the next sixty years or so wondering. And now he's been dead for a century, and I'll never know."

"Serena," Jaxon says.

"I loved him," I say, cutting him off. "I did. It might have been simple, but sometimes that's the best kind of love. But I was so angry that he had to think about it. When Renwick said I arrived at the academy with so much anger it made me one of the best, he meant it. I raged. I fought. I put everything I had into my training. Because I was so angry."

I look back up at Jaxon. "I spent a lot of time being angry. And for just a few moments, that night we met at the club, I wasn't angry. For a few moments these past few days, I've forgotten *why* I'm so angry."

We stare at each other, standing here in a kitchen far beneath the ground. And I don't doubt it, that he's also thinking about how unfair life truly is.

## Chapter Twelve

I HATE that I'm on a diurnal schedule now. After living in the LightVerse for so long, my brain has adjusted. I've had to learn to adapt. As much as I might miss the night, I cannot get the entire world to switch over to thriving in the dark.

When I wake up the next morning, it's with an idea rolling around my brain.

But I know no one is going to like it.

I climb out of bed and get dressed, then step out of my bedroom. I look through Jaxon's window, and find him still sleeping in his bed. So I head down the hall to find Davorian.

He's sitting in the command center with Nisha, and two other women.

It's been so long since I've seen them, that it takes me a good sixty seconds to recognize them.

"Serena, you remember our southeast agents," Davorian says as he looks back at me.

I slide my hands into my back pockets and nod to them. "Cordelia, and…Layla, right?"

"That's right," Layla says, and I'm both surprised and not when she talks with a Southern accent. They both have been stationed in the South for a very, very long time. They also covered Cuba, the Bahamas, and the surrounding region, but for the most part, they stayed in Alabama as their home base.

"They just arrived last night," Nisha says. She hardly even looks up as she works away on her screens. She is our coordinator, and she keeps everything under control with our organization. "We will have six more agents landing late tonight, all from the central America region. The rest will all be arriving over the next two weeks."

"It's been so long since we've all been together," I say, thinking back to the last time, more than 150 years ago. "It will be so strange to fill the compound up again."

"I kind of forgot what this place was like," Cordelia says. "It's…cozy. And dark."

She says it in a negative way.

And I wonder, when we get to go home, how hard is it going to be to adjust back?

I turn to Davorian. "Can I talk to you privately?"

None of the others blink an eye. They're used to this kind of chain of command.

He simply gives a nod, and we head into one of the offices. He closes the door behind us and we both sit at the table.

"I have an idea, or maybe it's more of a request, but I don't know that you're going to especially like it." I cross one leg over the other, leaning back in my chair. Davorian is my commander, he also happens to be twenty years my senior. But we've spent the majority of our lives working together, I respect him as my commander, but he is also my friend and comrade.

"What is it?" Davorian asks. His keen eyes are fixed on me, but he doesn't tense up. We trust each other.

"We are asking a lot of Jaxon, now that we know he is the gatekeeper," I say. "He's taking this all in stride, but I know that this can't feel real. He said he doesn't feel like this could possibly be real for him. He saw me shift, obviously he saw Ascelin and Renwick shift. And he saw when that Kindred attacked us, so he knows what the ultralights look like. But I don't think it's healthy for him to have only seen what he's going to be in the form of a Kindred. So..." I hesitate in my request, because I know how dangerous it is. In more ways than one. "I want to take him back into the city and let him observe the other ultralights as they work." I study Davorian's face once the words are out.

He's always had an excellent poker face. He keeps his expression smooth and calm, never once revealing how he truly feels about my request.

"We'll keep our distance," I say as my heart rate picks up just a little bit. "I'll never say I trust an ultralight, but out of all of them, I feel like the two that are operating here in Vegas are the best possible examples Jaxon could observe. I just think…that it would be good for him to see what his purpose really is. I've explained the Dusk to him, but it always just sounds like we're overreacting when I explain it. He doesn't really have an understanding of what it's really like. I think it would be good for him to see it."

I can see the gears turning in Davorian's head. He's mulling it over, weighing the benefits and the risks.

"And I think he needs to touch base with his family again," I move on with the rest of my plan. "He comes from a huge family, and it only took them two days to track us down when we were on the run. They're going to be looking for him. And while I don't think that they will ever find us here in the desert, it seems easier and safer to give them some sort of contact and establish a cover story. And I also think that it will make this transition easier. He will feel like less of a prisoner if we don't just stuff him down in the ground for the rest of his life. He is an ultralight after all. He's going to need some sunshine."

"And if he starts to manifest while you're out in the world?" Davorian asks.

"I'll be paying close attention, trust me," I say with a bit of a chuckle. I'm already on edge, waiting for that moment when heat starts to radiate from his body, and he starts to glow. I plan to be well out of the way, and make sure he's behind reinforced doors. No one is going to die, not on my watch. "And we won't be far."

Davorian looks down at the table and doesn't say anything for thirty long seconds. I don't envy his position. He's had to make a lot of impossible calls over all these years. I certainly wouldn't want to be the one making all of these life-or-death decisions.

"And we are both going to need to get some things from our homes," I move onto the last part of my plan. "I haven't lived in the compound for three years. But things have changed now. I need to go clean out my apartment and give up my lease. I need to get my bike and since my old car got blown up by the Kindred, I think I need to go shopping for a new one. Jaxon will be happier if he has some of his own things here."

Davorian holds my eyes for ten more seconds. I have a feeling I know what he's thinking.

We've found the gatekeeper. We're hoping to go home to the DarkVerse any moment now.

Am I really so sure it's going to take so long for the DarkVerse gatekeeper to come along that I'm worried about getting another car?

"I'm giving you twenty-four hours," he says. He lays one hand down flat on the table. "We're about to have a meeting, so we can talk about all the new security issues and all of the new needs we're going to have with all of the agents returning. I want you to leave then. Ascelin will have a coronary if he knows that I'm letting you two leave. Get out without anybody knowing. I'll deal with the rest of the fallout. And I mean it. Twenty-four hours, or you'll have half of the compound coming after the two of you. And I don't think it will be pretty."

I get up from my chair, not wanting to waste a single moment. "Thank you, Sir."

He simply nods and I turn and leave the room.

I don't waste any time. I head straight down the hall and knock on Jaxon's door twice before I let myself inside.

Jaxon rolls over with a sharp start. His fist balls up rising to action. With bleary, confused eyes he searches the space for the point of attack.

But when he sees it's just me, he lets his fist fall back to the bed.

"Get up," I say sharply. Even my voice is in a hurry. I know we haven't got much time to prepare for this. "Davorian has given us permission to leave the compound for a few hours. I figure it would be good to touch base with your family, and I thought you might want to grab a few of your things from your house. I need to get some from mine as well, and there's something I want to show you."

"Pretty sure that Ascelin guy is going to kill us if either of us tries to leave this place," Jaxon says, even as he stands and searches the space for his shirt.

I'm trying very, very hard not to stare at Jaxon as he stands, putting all of those muscles on beautiful display.

"We've got a small window of opportunity where he won't know," I say. "But we have to hurry."

I don't have to tell him twice. Jaxon finds his shirt lying across the chair in the corner. He tugs it over his head and over his body, sadly hiding everything he has to show. He slides his shoes on, and I go to the door, poking my head out and listening.

I hear Davorian's voice down the hall, but nothing else. He's already got his meeting started.

It's now or never.

I wave Jaxon out into the hall behind me. I hold one finger up to my lips indicating for him to be quiet. And silently, we make our way down towards the end of the hallway. All the way down to the opening above our heads.

"Don't scream," I say in the quietest voice that I can manage.

I kind of admire him that Jaxon only goes a little bit white when he nods.

I don't wait two more seconds before I let the

breath out, and all of my shadows take over my skin. Everything in me shifts, and I change form, change shape, change species.

Jaxon's eyes widen just a little bit as he watches me shift. But there's something new in his eyes when he sees me this time. I think I see something that almost represents…fascination. Maybe even…admiration.

I don't have time to evaluate it for long though. I reach out, grab Jaxon, and make my way up into the tunnel.

Jaxon is very still, but whereas before he shied away from my touch, he almost seems to lean into it, as if he is exploring the feel of it.

It's coming, and I hate it. As we climb higher and higher it suffocates me. The heat. The pounding of the sun.

But as we reach the surface, I hear Jaxon let out a relieved breath.

I set him down and instantly shift back into my human form.

He watches the entire time.

"You good if we take a bike?" I ask as I head to the rock formations to the side of the opening. "Considering my car got blasted apart when the Kindred attacked, we're going to have to go buy a new one today. I have a bike back at my apartment, but for now, were going to have to borrow Renwick's."

Jaxon smirks. "Oh, I think you know the answer to that question."

Without hesitating, he crosses over to the first motorcycle. He swings one leg over the beast. And I stop for just a second.

Jaxon, on a black motorcycle, is the most natural sight I have ever seen in my entire life.

"You got the keys?" he asks as he looks over his shoulder at me with that same smirk.

I can't help it. Something in my chest flutters with excitement and maybe something that feels a little bit like need. I smile myself. I reach into my pocket and I pull out the keys. I toss them to him and with nervous excitement climb onto the motorcycle behind him.

He roars the beast to life, and as he takes off, I grip him around the middle tightly.

I'm not going to fall off. As a darkling, my balance is exceptional.

I just really want to touch him.

Now that he knows where we are, Jaxon doesn't hesitate as he points the bike in the correct direction, and we rip over the red desert.

While it's noisy, the speed is high, and my hair whips out behind me, I take this moment to actually analyze what is going on right here.

I'm getting myself in trouble. With every day that is passing, I feel myself craving Jaxon's presence more and more. I find him occupying nearly every moment in my brain. I find myself craving his presence.

It's dangerous. Reckless.

He is an ultralight and I am a darkling.

But I've never been a particularly fearful person.

And I guess I've always craved just a little bit of danger.

So as we bullet across the desert, I wrap my arms around his waist a little tighter. And I lay my head between his shoulder blades, resting my front snugly to his back. And maybe I'm making it up in my head, but I swear he leans into me just slightly.

The sun is headed toward the peak of the sky when we reach the edge of the city. As we roll up to the main street, Jaxon pulls off into a gas station.

"Where to first?" he asks as he twists around and looks back at me.

"I need to swing by my apartment and grab some cash," I say. I don't let go of his waist. "I need to buy another car."

Jaxon simply nods, and for a moment, I look into his eyes.

Why does being with him, just the two of us, feel like…freedom?

I feel…wild when I'm with him. I feel lighter. I feel…normal.

But none of this is normal. We haven't really had any normal interactions since we met. Even that first night at the club wasn't real. I went there with the very intention to not be me that night.

So why do I feel like this when it's just me and him?

"Take a left up here," I say, nodding my head in that direction.

Jaxon revs the engine, and we pull back out onto the road.

I give him directions, weaving our way through the city, headed back toward the Strip. And just a block and a half out, I point to my building. I indicate my parking space and he pulls up behind my own motorcycle.

"Nice bike," Jaxon says as we climb off.

I just smirk and head up the stairs to the third floor.

"Serena."

I double back at the voice that calls out to me on the fourth floor.

Tim, the acrobat who is kind but too interested, steps out of his door. "You been out of town?"

I glance back at Jaxon, who looks at Tim with a wary expression. He doesn't trust much of anybody, and definitely not anybody in this town. "Yeah," I say as I look back at Tim. "I took a trip for a few days."

"Who's this?" he asks, nodding his head at Jaxon.

"My boyfriend," I say simply. And without waiting for any more questions or the disappointed look on his face, I grab Jaxon's hand and continue on up to the fifth floor.

I feel like I should be blushing when I catch Jaxon's eyes as I fish my keys out of my pocket.

But I'm not embarrassed.

Jaxon is absolutely my type, and I didn't even realize I had a type.

I would not be embarrassed if he was my boyfriend.

The doorknob twists and I push it open, the both of us stepping inside.

There's this feeling of…disappointment that fills me when I look around my apartment. And also…detachment.

There was an era of my life when I needed this place. When I needed my own space. I needed time to grieve the fact that I was never returning home.

But my facts are not entirely facts.

"I think I pictured something a little more glamourous," Jaxon says as he looks around. "You're this ultra badass. I was expecting some kind of shiny, black lair."

I chuckle as I head to the closet. I push aside my clothes and reach for the envelope taped to the underside of a shelf. I pull it out and set it on the bed as I pull my jacket off. "Guess the décor here fits the mood of when I signed the lease. I was accepting the underbelly life of living in Las Vegas."

"What's that supposed to mean?" he asks as he sinks onto my bed. Considering this is a studio apartment, everything is exposed, all in once space, except for the bathroom.

I turn to the closet and dig around for a different shirt. The one I'm wearing is three years old and my style has changed since. With my back to Jaxon, I pull the one I'm wearing off.

"I mean, as a darkling always on the hunt for the gatekeeper and with ultralights constantly floating in and out of the area, we can't exactly hold a job." I grab a tank top toward the back. It's high necked, but the sides are open, with a thick black tie crisscrossing in a pattern up both sides. I pull it over my head and strip my old jeans off. "It means that a few of us have to get creative in financially supporting the compound."

I hear Jaxon clear his throat, but it sounds strange, a little strangled.

I look over my shoulder. He's staring at me, and there is no shame in his eyes. He takes me in. All of me. And I can tell, he likes what he sees.

I can't help but smile as I turn back to the closet and search through the options for a pair of shiny, breathable black pants. I pull them on up, wiggling my hips to get them up.

Now I really am blushing when I turn around. Jaxon's eyes are hungry, and I really, really like the look in them.

"I'm constantly in and out of the different casinos," I explain instead of paying attention to the heat in my lower belly. "In the 158 years I've been in Vegas, I've learned a few tricks. And the methods to not draw attention."

"You support the entire compound with your gambling?" Jaxon asks, his tone impressed.

"Not just me," I say. "Renwick and Philomena do it, too. Let's just say we're good enough that we only have to go out a few nights a year to keep up the cash stores."

I reach under the bed and pull out another envelope taped to the bottom of the bedframe.

Something lights in Jaxon's eyes as I smile. Something that recognizes this type of lifestyle. I see... mischief in his eyes.

"This should do it," I say. "We'll stop back by here later for the rest of my stuff. But first, it's time for a new car."

He huffs a little laugh, and I can't help but smile. I feel as if the real Jaxon is coming through right now. He's relaxing, loosening up, showing me his less guarded self.

We head back down the stairs, and when I spot Tim down below, his eyes watching for my return, I reach back and slide my fingers through Jaxon's. I lean into him just a little.

I internally sigh. Even his scent is driving me crazy.

"Have a good one, Tim," I call as we pass his level.

He looks a little defeated as he waves to us, and we continue on down.

I don't let go of Jaxon's hand. He doesn't try to pull away.

I pull out the keys to my bike and hop on. Jaxon settles into the seat behind me. As I rev the engine to life, he places his hands on my hips, and I like the way it feels way, way too much.

I navigate my way to the dealership I have in mind, one that doesn't ask too many questions and always has nice cars. When I park out in front of the sales office, I hear Jaxon give a little laugh.

"What?" I ask as we both climb off of my bike.

"It's just that I might know the owner of this place," he says, even as the door to the office swings open and a heavy, balding man walks out.

He makes this little terrified squeaking sound. "Mr. Gray," he says, and his face blanches stark white. "I don't…it isn't the end of the month yet. I—"

"Relax, Billy," Jaxon says. There's this look on his face, one of confidence and control. It's even in the way he walks as he takes a step forward to my side. "I'm not here for you. My girlfriend is just looking for a new car."

I'm starting to get way too used to this name-calling game.

"For you, thirty percent off any window price," Billy says, his words coming out fast. He's wearing this awkward, forced smile, when I can see in his eyes that he's terrified.

My eyes slide over to Jaxon, who just gives a little shrug. I smile and turn to survey the options.

An hour later, I roll out of the parking lot in a glossy, slick black car with less than five thousand miles on it. It's titled under my fake ID, no questions asked. It's the quickest and most hassle-free car purchase in the history of any human.

Jaxon follows behind me on my bike, back to my apartment. Together, we pack up all of my things, which really isn't a whole lot. The studio came furnished with everything I needed, which was another reason why I signed the lease. So, we fill two duffle bags and two boxes full of my things and load them into the trunk.

Tim watches from his window as we load my things up. He doesn't come out and ask what's going on. I told him Jaxon was my boyfriend. When your boyfriend helps you move your things out, it's pretty easy to assume what's going on.

Tim fully believes I'm moving in with Jaxon.

I guess in a way, he's not wrong.

"How bad of an idea is it to go by your place and get whatever you need?" I ask when we close the trunk.

Jaxon's gaze automatically swings toward the casino his family lives in. "Probably a good and bad idea," he says. "My family will start getting suspicious again if I don't show my face. But my brothers did say Mom had a job for me today. It might be hard to get out of that one."

I nod. I'm not really sure what to do about that, and I'm not really sure what other option we're going to have with it. Not if we want to make this smooth.

"K, we'll leave the bikes here for now. My lease expires next week anyway, so the place is still technically mine for a bit longer. I'll send Philomena and Ren after them tonight, after it's dark. They'll get here quick under cover."

He nods and opens the passenger door. I slip in the car, and we back out of my space.

He doesn't have to navigate me to the right place. I remember it very clearly, that day I followed him, when he showed up on our radar.

I park in the parking garage and look over at him.

"You're kind of part of my cover story," Jaxon says. He looks up at me hesitantly from beneath his thick blond eyelashes with those intense green eyes. "They'll buy it easier if you're with me."

I just nod, and we both climb out.

He holds the door to the building open for me and we step inside.

It already smells like cigarettes and despair.

Jaxon takes my hand in his and we cross to the elevators. He hits the up button, and we wait.

He seems…nervous. He's so quiet, and his eyes are

intensely fixed on the closed doors in front of us. He isn't sure what to expect. And I have a feeling that he knows he's going to have to do his mother's bidding, and he doesn't exactly love the family legacy.

Just before the doors slide open with a ding, I give his hand a reassuring squeeze.

We step inside and he presses the button for the fifteenth floor.

Chapter Thirteen

THE ELEVATOR OPENS, and we both stop a little short when a woman is standing there, stepping forward without waiting for it to clear.

"Jaxon," she says, her eyes a little wide. "Where the hell have you been?"

Still hand in hand, we both step off the elevator. The woman puts her hand out, keeping it open, so at least we won't have to be in this conversation for long.

"Why does everyone suddenly want me around so bad?" Jaxon says, feigning annoyance. "Can't a guy just get a few days away with his new girl?"

The woman's expression changes from annoyed to surprised. She looks a touch older than Jaxon, but I recognize her from AJ's funeral.

"Girlfriend?" she asks, surprised. "You? It's been, what? Three years?"

"Shut up," Jaxon says, and it's both teasing and serious. "Chantel, this is Serena. Serena, Chantel."

"Nice to meet you," Chantel says, even as she walks into the elevator. "Mom's pretty ticked at you. But maybe it will butter her up that you're bringing a girl home."

She smiles just as the elevator doors close.

"What's it like, growing up with six siblings?" I ask. "I only had one younger brother, but he died of a fever when he was only two."

Jaxon looks over at me, and I think he realizes the difference in time that I'm talking about. A fever wouldn't be a big deal now. But in the mid-eighteen hundreds, it was an entirely different story.

"I don't think what it was for me was what it would have been for anyone else," Jaxon says as we hurry down the hall, my hand still in his. "For me, it just meant there was always someone to fight with, someone to pick on, someone to get in trouble with. We've never been…close."

We pass the door his family congregated behind that night. Jaxon walks past it and down two more doors.

Instead of the normal hotel key swipe entry, this one has a keypad. Jaxon quickly punches in a series of six numbers. It clicks, and he pushes it open.

It's the equivalent of a large hotel room. It's decorated modern and moody. There's a huge king-sized bed pushed against one wall. There's a massively tall, padded black headboard at the head of it. A white comforter is laid on it, with big, fluffy white pillows. The walls are decorated starkly black and white, matching the shiny black marble floors.

It's almost cliché.

"Probably better to pack now, so no one realizes how much stuff I'm grabbing," he says as he walks inside. I follow him, taking it all in.

Jaxon heads straight into a closet and begins filling a duffel bag. I smile as I take note that everything inside that closet is black and white.

But I leave him to it. There's a wall of glass opposite the bed, and it looks out with a spectacular view of the Strip.

It's July, so the heat is intense and the sun is so bright I feel as if my eyeballs are being seared. It's quiet down on the streets. No one wants to be out in this 108-degree heat.

Unnatural. Why would people choose to live in a place that's constantly trying to kill them?

Just five minutes later, Jaxon walks out of the bathroom with his bag over his shoulder.

"That should do it," he says. "I…" He takes a deep breath, and his eyes rise to the ceiling. I can tell how badly he doesn't want to do this next part.

"Let's go meet your family," I say. I want to ease his anxiety and dread. I want to brush my thumbs over the furrows between his eyebrows. I want to run my hand down the back of his neck, press my forehead to his, and suggest that we both just disappear without a trace.

Instead, I take a step forward, and reach for his hand.

There's a look of peace that settles into his eyes as he takes it. Together, we walk to the door.

He leaves his duffle bag just inside. It will be ready to retrieve as soon as we get to leave.

Hand in hand, we walk back down the hall. He hesitates outside the door for two seconds.

And then he punches in the code. It beeps, and he pushes it open.

Even though we're not on the top floor of this casino, I would still call this a penthouse. We step into a large living area, decorated lavishly in shades of gray and black. There's a long, slick black dining table with twelve chairs around it. To the back, there is a kitchen with slick black cabinets and stark white countertops. Floor to ceiling windows give the same view Jaxon's room has.

I see a bedroom branching off to the left, and the door to what looks to be an office. I hear the sound of two chairs being pushed back from inside it, and a moment later, Blake steps out, followed immediately by a woman I recognize from the funeral.

So this is the mother I've heard so much about.

"You've finally returned home," she says as she casually walks into the room, stopping just a few feet in front of us.

"Mom," Jaxon says with an acknowledging nod. "Serena, this is my mother, Vivian Gray. Mom, this is my girlfriend, Serena."

I wonder then if Jaxon realizes that he doesn't even know my last name. What he certainly doesn't know is that I haven't used that last name since I got marooned in the LightVerse. Because it hasn't mattered since then.

If I'm being honest with myself, I can't even remember exactly what it was. Time has a way of erasing trivial details.

"It's an honor to meet you, Miss Gray," I say as I take a step forward and extend a hand. I gather every ounce of confidence I have, funneling it into my voice, my body language.

I'm not afraid of Vivian Gray. Not one bit.

But right now, I have to play a part. I have to be someone believable who would be with Jaxon, who can stand on her own two feet in this world.

"Pleasure," she says. Her eyes are cold and evaluating.

Vivian Gray is at once elegant and intimidating. She's well dressed, wearing stylish black pants and a sleeveless white shirt with a high neck. Her hair is a tad darker than Jaxon's, closer to Aaron's or Chantel's shade. Her makeup is done well, making her look younger than I think she really is, but then she wears brilliant red lipstick that hints at the dangerous woman she is.

"My apologies for being a bit distracted the last week," Jaxon says, moving along. And for a second, I think I need to correct him. It has to have been multiple weeks now. But as I think back on it, it truly has only been nine days. "I certainly wasn't expecting to get so…enamored," he says as he looks back over at me. His eyes are hungry, even his mouth is set in this position of lust. He looks me up and down, and heat rushes over my entire body.

*This is all for show,* I internally tell myself.

But deep down, I know that not all of it is fake.

"I simply find myself surprised," Vivian says. Slowly, a smile begins pulling on those red lips. "It's been a long time since you've even looked at a woman. You…" she trails off as her eyes study her son. "You seem…happy."

Jaxon hasn't looked away from me this whole time, and he doesn't look away now. I see something soften in his expression, and the look in his eyes turns genuine. "I am," he says simply.

The smile seems real when Vivian takes a step forward and she pulls me into a hug. "If you can make my Jaxon this happy, you are welcome in my home."

But even as she hugs me, it feels as if I am embracing a panther.

"Come, let's sit," she says as she backs away. She extends a hand out to the seating area.

Jaxon takes my hand once again, and I can already feel the tension in him once more.

We settle into the gray leather couch, and I make sure to sit close, tucking myself into Jaxon's side. He extends one arm along the back of the couch, behind my neck, and he gently takes my hand with his other.

Vivian settles into one of the severely modern seats across from us, Blake taking the other.

"So, how did you two meet?" Vivian asks.

A man that I can describe no other way than a butler, walks into the living area. He takes a bottle of wine from a cupboard and walks over with several glasses. Vivian and Blake both take one. I shake my head at it, as does Jaxon.

"The club," Jaxon explains honestly. "The night I was looking for Aaron."

"Some guy at the bar was being a misogynist," I say, letting a little smile curl on my lips. "Jaxon walked up and pretended to be someone I was waiting for."

"Because I was pretty sure if someone didn't intervene immediately she was going to murder the guy right there and then."

I smile, remembering how truly angry I did feel

that night. And then how relieved I was when Jaxon stepped in.

"What a gentleman," Vivian says, her tone measured and even, though a slight smile pulls on her face. "What a strong woman. Tell me, Serena, what is it you do for a living?"

"Personal security," I spout out without even hesitating.

Sort of true. I am a guardian. Just…of the entire DarkVerse.

"I guess none of us should be surprised that Jaxon found himself a woman who can handle herself," Blake says. I don't like his leering gaze, as his eyes drop down my entire body, head to foot.

"We respect strong women in this family," Vivian says, and the words are genuine. She says it with a warning side glace at her eldest son. "I'm pleased Jaxon has found one of them."

I give an appreciative nod.

"We're heading out again," Jaxon says. His tone gets a little louder, there's a touch more confidence forced into it. "I want to meet Serena's family. They live in North Dakota. We're…" he glances over at me, and his eyes drop from mine, to my lips, and then back up to mine again. "We're going to elope, but I thought it was only proper that I meet her family first." He looks back at his mother. "Out of respect."

Jaxon is good at this. He is an exceptional liar. Even

I believe it, that we really are eloping and that he wants to meet my family, out of respect.

Too bad they've been dead for over a century.

"Eloping?" Vivian says, her eyebrows raising a touch. "You're ready to commit a lifetime so soon?"

Jaxon looks down at our hands laced together. "There isn't a bone in my body that believes I'll find anyone more intriguing than Serena. I want to be with her." He looks up at his mother again. "More than anything."

Vivian doesn't say anything for a moment, just holds her son's gaze. I wonder how good she is at reading liars. I would guess very, considering what she does for a living.

But Jaxon is the best liar I've ever met in my life.

"Well, then who am I to stand in the way of my son's happiness?" she says. Another of her small, controlled smiles curls on her lips. "Go meet your future bride's family. We look forward to a wedding soon. Would you like to have it here, at the hotel?"

Jaxon looks over at me, and I see a spark of excitement in his eyes—this is working. "We…haven't really discussed that part yet."

"What, you haven't worked through your life plan together after the nine days you've known each other?" Blake teases.

"How's Melanie?" Jaxon fires off without missing a beat.

With Blake's stunned silence, and the dark, hard look that takes over his face, I know Jaxon has struck a nerve.

Something tingles in me when Jaxon smirks.

He has a dimple on either side of his mouth.

"I do have a job for you to do before you depart," Vivian says as she crosses one leg over the other. "You've been so successful in getting the Ramirez family caught up on their debts, I hate to throw a wrench in the cogs and send Griff instead. I need you to pay them a visit before you leave. Now would be ideal."

It's obvious. Vivian is not a woman you say no to. She is not a woman her children say no to.

And if we're going to get out of this situation without drawing any unwanted attention, Jaxon cannot say no.

I feel it. The stiffness in Jaxon's shoulders. The way his hand tightens around mine. He knows what this job is going to entail.

He doesn't want to do it. But there is no other choice.

"I'm headed there now," he says. "And we'll take off from there."

Jaxon stands and pulls me to my feet beside him. He pulls me in close, letting his hand come to my lower back. My *very* lower back. Vivian rises as well and we all head toward the door.

"It was a pleasure meeting you, Serena," she says. I think she means it, but it's hard to tell. "I look forward to getting to know my soon to be daughter-in-law better."

"And you as well, Miss Gray," I say with a little nod.

It says something about her that she does not ask me to call her Vivian.

Jaxon opens the door and pulls me out into the hall with him.

We walk fifteen steps before he turns and braces his forearm against the wall, and rests his forehead against it. He takes in four sharp breaths between his teeth.

"After today, it'll all be over," I say. Instinctively, I place my hand on his back, a gesture of reassurance. "You'll never have to see her, or them again, if you don't want to."

I step just a little closer, and I know I shouldn't, but I can't help it when my arms wrap around his middle and I hug myself into his back. "I can keep you safe from them."

Jaxon looks back at me over his shoulder. The moment is heavy and loaded, like we're just waiting for something to explode, for the cannon to be fired.

But it's there in the back of his mind, and it's certainly in the back of mine.

Hours. Days.

Not long now, and he'll want to kill me with every instinct in his body.

He takes one of my hands and raises it. He presses his lips to the back of my hand.

It just about kills me, when he lowers it and I have to let go of him. But we have somewhere to be.

So we retrieve Jaxon's bag from his room, and then we're back in the elevator, headed for the car.

## Chapter Fourteen

I DON'T ASK QUESTIONS. I let Jaxon take the driver's seat, considering I have no idea where this Ramirez family lives. He drives us to the south end of town. We pull past huge houses with gates surrounding them. Expensive cars sit out in driveways, an obvious show of wealth. None of these people would leave their vehicles outside the garage without them being home.

The road dead ends at a particularly huge house. It sprawls side to side, the landscaping extravagant. They even have real grass. The house is a Spanish mission style with a grand clay tile roof.

Jaxon rolls up into the middle of their roundabout driveway and parks right in front of the door.

"This might get ugly," he says as he reaches into his bag. He pulls out a handgun and tucks it into the back of his pants. "Stay back here."

I shake my head. "Not a chance," I say. "Now that we know you're the gatekeeper, I'm not letting you walk into any dangerous situations alone. I'm not ready to live through that hell."

The hell of just finding him, only to have him get killed like his brother was, and then spend another century looking for the next gatekeeper.

"Promise you won't have to worry about me," I say as I bat my eyelashes and flash him a bright, fake smile.

Jaxon just chuckles and climbs out of the car. I get out after him and follow him up to the front doors.

Jaxon pounds on the door twice, loudly. Loud enough to get attention. And then he reaches for the doorknob and twists. When it gives, he pushes the door open, and strides in without hesitating.

"Antonio!" he calls out, loudly. I'm impressed how his voice fills the entire grand entry way. He sounds aggressive, terrifying. "Mom needs her money, Antonio."

When we hear the sound of running footsteps upstairs, Jaxon streaks up them, taking them two at a time. I'm two steps behind him.

We barrel down a hallway and Jaxon drops his shoulder and busts straight through a door.

I step through, just in time to see a man slipping out the window.

I half shift, skittering across the room on eight legs. I grip him around the ankle and yank him back inside.

Just as he hits the floor, I once more shift back into fully human form.

"Where you going, Antonio?" Jaxon says as he crosses the room. He kneels on the man's chest, placing his hand on the man's throat. He shoves him back, hard, and his head thunks against the hardwood floors. "You aren't trying to bag out on your debt, are you? Because you know how well that worked out for you brother. Did you ever find all the pieces of Julio?"

The man gives a gargling squeak before he's cut off as Jaxon thunks his head back again.

"Don't give me any excuses, Antonio," Jaxon says as he shakes his head. "See, I'm kind of in a hurry. I don't really want to be here. You're kind of putting a kink in my day. See this woman here?"

Antonio's eyes shift over to me. I just give him a pretty smile and wave at him.

"I told Mom that I'm headed out to meet her family, so we can elope next week," Jaxon says, and something pulls at my insides. He doesn't have to tell this lie to Antonio. "And I'm definitely ready to get out of Vegas. So just be a good boy and go get me my money, so we can be on our way."

Antonio's face is turning beet red from how much pressure Jaxon is putting on his throat. He barely manages a nod. Jaxon releases his throat and stands. He extends a hand to Antonio to help him to his feet.

But Antionio just glares at him, and makes his way to his feet on his own.

It's obvious how many times Jaxon has done this before. He walks right behind Antonio, barely giving him more than an arm's length of space between the two of them.

Antonio crosses to the closet in this bedroom. He pulls the doors open, and he reaches for something near the back.

My instincts here in the LightVerse are not what they are in the DarkVerse. But still, every now and then, I just know.

The hair on the back of my neck stands on end.

All of my senses go into overdrive.

And the monster inside of me comes out.

I roll forward as I shift instantly. I shove Jaxon out of the way with my legs, and roll right into Antonio's way, just as he turns around, and swings forward with a knife.

It embeds itself in my shadows, and he immediately gives a terrified scream as he realizes what he's facing.

A demonic howl radiates from my fangs, right in his face. One of my pincers rises up, and I yank the knife from my form.

I see Jaxon move from the corner of one of my eyes. He grabs a lamp from a nightstand and takes a swing.

It hits Antonio in the back of the head, and he drops instantly, falling into me, and then collapsing on the floor.

I shift back into human form and take a step back.

"You okay?" Jaxon asks. His tone is panicked. He's instantly in front of me, searching for the injury where the blade stabbed me.

I'm still coming down from the high of the shift. I look down at myself, internally searching for where it hurts.

My thigh starts throbbing and as I reach down, I find blood seeping through my pants.

"Where?" Jaxon asks, his hands hovering over me.

"Here," I hiss, stepping back and sitting on the padded bench at the foot of the bed. "Is he dead?"

"Who the hell cares?" Jaxon spits as he kneels in front of me. And I'm shocked when he reaches for the waistband of my pants and yanks down. Every nerve ending in my body decides to go haywire. Jaxon's eyes scrape down my legs, and he goes a little paler when he sees the stab wound in my thigh. He swears.

"Stay there," he commands. "I'm sure he's got some kind of medical supplies in this house. These types usually do. Does that need stitches?"

I push on the wound, trying to tell how deep it is. I see down into muscle and fat. "Yep."

Jaxon just nods once, and without saying another word, he steps out of the bedroom to search the house.

I lean forward and look down at Antonio. He's not bleeding, which is surprising. It was a pretty hard hit to the head he took. I stare at his chest for four long seconds, waiting to see it move.

Finally, it rises, and then slowly, it falls.

He'll probably have a wicked concussion, but at least he isn't dead.

Jaxon fully admitted to me that he killed Carley's kidnapper. Shot him right between the eyes.

I find myself hoping he never has to kill anyone else ever again. Especially not on my behalf.

My eyes turn up to the closet in front of me, and I search.

There, on the top shelf, is a small safe. And I have no doubt Vivian's money is inside it.

Jaxon walks back in then, a first aide kit clutched in his left hand. He sets it on the bench beside me and kneels in front of me.

"This is going to hurt like hell," he says as he pulls out some cotton balls and hydrogen peroxide. "But I wouldn't trust any knife of Antonio's to be clean."

He pours a healthy amount into the cotton and then wipes it over the stab wound.

A hiss rips from my lips and I reach out, grabbing Jaxon's shoulders. My grip must be deadly. Jaxon winces, but he doesn't pull away.

"One more, okay?" he says as his eyes rise up to meet mine. There's regret in his eyes, maybe even shame. But I can tell he's done this kind of thing before.

I just nod and get myself ready for the next wave of pain.

I hiss again, and grip Jaxon so hard, I know I'll bruise him. But it's over in just a couple of seconds and then he's blowing on it gently, trying to sooth the burn.

"You didn't have to do that," Jaxon says as he reaches into the kit for a needle and thread. "I've dealt with guys with knives before, trust me."

"You could just say thank you," I snap, hissing as he digs the needle into my skin for the first time.

Instantly, his eyes snap back up to mine. "I didn't mean… Thank you, Serena."

He means it, and instantly everything in me softens. "I still get these…feelings sometimes. I don't have a purpose here in the LightVerse, but still, every now and then, I just get these urges, similar to what I got in the DarkVerse. I can just tell bad things are about to happen. That's the feeling I just got. I don't know how far it would have gone, Jaxon, but it would have been bad." I swallow, watching as he threads the needle through my skin again, wiping away the blood as he works. "I couldn't let anything happen to you."

He stills at my words, and he looks up at me again. And I see something in his eyes. Something that feels familiar. Something that says he's thinking the same thing.

The gash is only two and a half inches long, so it only takes Jaxon two or three minutes to stitch it up. This moment takes me back to the hotel room, that first night I grabbed him and ran. When I stitched up his face in the flickering light in the bathroom. Those stitches are still in his face right now.

"It's almost easy to imagine this is going to be our new normal," I say. I don't mean to speak them out loud, but they're through my lips before my brain can stop them. "Us doing dangerous stuff together, stitching each other up after."

Jaxon looks up at me, and we simply look at each other for a long time.

It's really, really easy to imagine it. We work well together, and we haven't really even tried. All this time since the darklings have been trapped in the Light-Verse, we work as a unit, but we're always working on our own. I've never wanted a partner with me on a regular basis.

But with Jaxon, it's easy to imagine. Us working together, fighting together, shifting together.

I shouldn't imagine it so much.

But from the look in his eyes, I can tell he's doing the exact same thing.

"Those stitches need to come out," I say. My fingers rise and touch his temple lightly. "Come on, I'll take them out for you."

He stands and holds a hand out for me. I take it and test my weight on my leg. I've had worse. I'll live.

He grabs my pants from the floor and the first aid kit from the bench, and we both go into the connected bathroom.

My heartrate quickens when he sets the kit down and goes straight for the sink. He turns the water on cold and puts the bloody part of my pants under, scrubbing the fabric together.

It's weird, seeing my blood stain his hands. It's weird seeing the concerned look furrowing the space between his brows.

It's weird standing next to him in nothing but my underwear but feeling entire comfortable.

It's weird how my chest is aching, harder and harder, every single day.

It's going to kill me, being around him every day, feeling this feeling, but not being able to be with him the way we have in the past nine days.

*Be here, right now,* I tell myself. *In this moment. Appreciate it while it's here.*

Jaxon finishes rinsing the blood out of my pants. "Wait here," he says. I just nod and listen as he walks out and starts opening and closing doors. A moment later, I hear the sound of a dryer starting.

He walks back in a few seconds later. He leans back against the counter, and hands me the needle-nosed scissors.

"I'm sorry," he says as he braces his hands back against the counter. I reach up and clip the first thread. "I never meant for you to get hurt."

I shrug. "You live this long, you're bound to get a few scrapes and bruises." I clip the next thread, and carefully tug it out.

"Still," he says. "I'm sorry. This life I've lived…"

"I'm okay, Jaxon," I say, cutting him off. "Trust me, I've lived through worse. I'm just glad you weren't hurt. You'll be tougher when you manifest, but for now, I just… I don't mind."

His green eyes meet mine, and for a second, I pause in pulling his stitches.

All the alarm bells are going off in my brain.

But everything in me is rising up, surging, and I don't know if I have the strength to fight the tide.

"We should get out of here before Antonio wakes up," I say as I pull out the last thread. "There is a safe in that closet. I can get it open. Seems likely the money is in there."

Jaxon swallows once and nods. He leaves the first aid kit on the counter, and the threads from his face. There are still splashes of blood on the counter and in the sink. But he's obviously not inclined to clean up our mess.

We step back into the bedroom. I step over Antonio, who is still breathing on the floor. I reach for the safe, and let my shadows slip out through my fingers.

I turn the dial with the other hand and feel for the clicks as the locks slide into place.

In sixty seconds, the last lock clicks into place, and I pull it open.

Just like a good little gambler, there are three big stacks of cash laying right there.

I step aside and let Jaxon count through what his family is owed.

He takes the vast majority of the money there and slips it all into his back pocket. "Come on," he says. "Let's get out of here."

I look down at Antonio once more as I step over his sleeping form. *Sleep well*, I think to him.

We retrieve my pants from the dryer. They're still damp, but considering the sweltering heat outside, they'll be dry in no time.

Jaxon only half looks away as I pull them on and slide them up and over my hips.

Thirty seconds later, we're walking back down the stairs. Jaxon locks the front door behind us, and we get back in the car.

"I want to show you what a normal ultralight does," I say as I pull my phone out, sitting in the driver's seat. "They're not all maniacs who only want to kill darklings. Most of them go about their lives, doing what they've evolved to do."

I tap on the icon that brings up our satellite

imagery. I show Jaxon as I zoom in, dropping us closer and closer in on Las Vegas.

There are three glowing dots on the screen. One, right here in this car. The other two are back in town, on the Strip, already at it for the day.

"There are two ultralights that live here in Vegas," I say. "They live, have normal jobs, have a semi-normal life dating and visiting family and everything. But they track down the Dusk, and they exorcise it, just as they're supposed to. I thought that it might be good for you to see it yourself. What you'll be able to do. How it works."

"I assume you mean incognito?" he asks, raising an eyebrow.

"Of course," I say.

He takes a deep breath, and I wonder what's going through his head. So far, the only ultralight he's seen was the Kindred who tried to kill me. I can understand why he's nervous, or doubtful.

But he just nods his head. So I put the car into drive, and we pull out of Antonio's driveway.

I throw my phone's screen onto the car's display and navigate my way toward the Strip.

They're together. They usually are if they're working. This isn't a busy time of day when the possessed come out. That's generally the nighttime. So we're lucky. It's not quite even dinner time, and they're already out and about.

We work our way down the Strip, one stoplight at a time. The two glowing dots grow closer, but then take a sharp turn down a side street. I turn left and follow after them.

I've actually never been in this part of town. It's kind of an industrial area. There are restaurant supply signs around. But I turn a corner and see the way down an alley, where delivery trucks would normally come early in the mornings. For now, it's quiet, totally abandoned.

I park in an inconspicuous space and double check the imagery.

Just then, a back door opens, and a man goes tumbling through it. He gives an angry, yet terrified yell as he rolls back, feet going over his head before he lands flat on his stomach.

Two women storm out of the doors behind him.

The second they're outside, their eyes glow brilliant white. Their hands ignite into white flames. Their very skin glows brilliant, as if they're so full of light, it's about to burst out of their skin.

I look over at Jaxon, making sure he's seeing all of this.

He stares at them, his mouth slightly open, his eyes wide and fixed.

The man tries to skitter back from them, and already I can see the warring emotions on his face.

He's possessed. He hasn't embraced the Dusk yet,

or he wouldn't look conflicted. He'd merely be angry beyond all reason.

He'd be fighting them with every last breath in him.

The two women stalk forward, coming on either side of him. One reaches forward and grabs him by the shoulders.

The other woman steps forward. And with her glowing hands, she reaches forward.

I listen for Jaxon's reaction when her hands sink right into the man's chest…when she gets wrist deep in his chest cavity.

He makes a noise, one of shock and maybe disgust. But I don't look at his face. I can't look away. Because this part is what I miss. My purpose. My reason for being what I am.

I can do that, even here in the LightVerse, but I just can't tell who has been possessed.

The woman digs around in the man's chest and he squirms in agony. But not because she's physically hurting him. Because the Dusk is being ripped from his soul.

She suddenly yanks her hand out of his chest. There, in her hand, is a swirling gray mass of…nothingness.

She holds it caged between her hands. The look on her face hardens. She grits her teeth. And her hands glow brighter and brighter.

Jaxon grips the center arm rest. His fingers grip tighter and tighter. His knuckles go white.

With one last surge of brilliant light, the Dusk dissolves, obliterated into nothingness.

It's instinctual. They haven't seen me. But as soon as the threat of the Dusk is eliminated, both of the ultralights' eyes snap up to me.

I throw the car into reverse, and I back up, barely missing a guy in a ridiculous chef's hat walking on the sidewalk.

"Are they…?" Jaxon asks in a panic as I put the car into drive.

"No," I say, though I'm only fifty percent sure. "The two of them know about us here. We've had encounters before. Instincts kick in, but they're not focused on eliminating us. There's enough of the Dusk around in this area to keep them occupied.

Jaxon turns around and looks out the back window. I glance in the rearview mirror.

Both women walk out into the road. Their hands are still glowing just slightly as they look after us.

But neither of them takes off after us.

I don't even slow at the stop sign. I just pull out and turn right.

## Chapter Fifteen

We make the drop. It's not like I expect. I kind of thought we'd go back to the casino and hand the money over in a crumpled up paper bag. But Jaxon guides us to a bank a half mile away. We walk inside and Jaxon asks for Mr. Royal.

A tall man with severe features comes out. He is stony faced and serious. We go to a private office. Mr. Royal counts out the cash. Without saying a word, he enters the deposit into his system. He prints out a receipt and hands it over to Jaxon.

We leave without saying anything else. Not a single word spoken between Jaxon and Mr. Royal.

As soon as we're back in the car, Jaxon snaps a picture of the receipt and texts it to his mother.

"Now what?" Jaxon asks as he relaxes back into his seat. And it's actually kind of amazing. It is almost like seeing a literal and physical weight lift off of his shoulders now that he's finished what he had to do for his mother. "We've got at least a week before my family bothers us again. So, now what?"

My chest is growing tighter by the moment. We've accomplished everything I'd been given permission to do when we left the compound. If I was being responsible, we should be heading back as soon as possible. Every moment I'm in danger out here, because Jaxon really is going to manifest any second.

But I really, truly can't bring myself to go back right now. Back to where they all will be watching us with hawks' eyes. To where I'm just so full of dread, because everything is about to change.

"You hungry?" I ask as I look over at him.

A smile spreads on his face, and I know just how much trouble I'm in. "I'm starving."

I try to suppress my own smile as I put the car into drive, but I don't succeed.

There certainly is a plethora of options for amazing food in Las Vegas. I run through my brain, thinking of my favorites. It's been a hobby of mine over the past couple of decades, to find all the best food in this dry town. I aim us for one on the Strip, and then pull into their parking garage.

I feel time ticking as we climb out. I feel it passing by too quick, one second at a time.

Our moments together are slipping away, and it's

making me feel desperate.

So, just after we step inside the doors, I slide my hand into Jaxon's. He looks down at our hands, studying them for three long seconds, and then he looks where we're walking again. And I think that look on his face is maybe peace.

We wander through the casino to the restaurant I have in mind. We wait for a few minutes until it's our turn to step up to the host.

I don't mind.

I find myself leaning into Jaxon. I breathe in his scent, which has constantly been swirling through my mind in the past week and a half.

He leans in close to me. His chest brushes mine. There is no space between his thigh and mine.

My blood is racing with anticipation.

And then it's our turn.

"Table for the couple?" the host asks, smiling warmly at us.

"Yes, please," Jaxon answers.

The man nods, grabs two menus, and waves for us to follow him.

Jaxon doesn't let go of my hand. Not once.

"So, are we celebrating anything tonight?" the host asks as we weave our way through booths and tables.

"We're celebrating nine days since we met," Jaxon says without hesitating.

That throws the host off. He raises an eyebrow and

offers a wary smile.

But this is Vegas, after all. A lot of couples in this situation would already be married and annulled by this point.

"Here we are," he says, laying the menus on the table, a private booth at the back of the restaurant. One single light hangs over the center of the table, casting a dim, red glow over the space.

Jaxon lets me slide into the booth first, and then follows after me.

He doesn't sit any further away from me than necessary.

My heart is hammering. My stomach is fluttering. I'm really not hungry, but I'll take any excuse I possibly can to have just a few more stolen moments alone.

Jaxon takes his menu and reads it from top to bottom, so I make myself do the same, force myself to concentrate on the words in front of my face.

When the waiter comes, I order a lemonade and something with chicken in it.

Jaxon leans an elbow on the table and looks at me. He takes his time studying me. My eyes, my hair, my lips.

So, I do the same.

He really is so beautiful, in the roughest way possible.

His hair is pulled back in a messy knot at the base of his neck. Small strands of it have escaped, curling at his temples. It's naturally curly, but in a very inconsistent way. Certain streaks of it are much lighter than others. Actually, his hair kind of looks like he belongs on a beach with a surfboard.

He hasn't had access to a razor in a few days, so there's a coating of scruff on his jaw. I kind of like it.

His green eyes are intense. I love the way they look when he's looking at me.

One stitch at a time, I feel myself being tied to him just a little more. Second by second, I'm losing my separation.

And I can't stop it. I don't care to stop it.

Maybe I have more self-destructive tendencies than I thought.

"So where do we go from here?" he asks. I can tell he's asking in more ways than one.

But I go for simple. "Davorian gave us twenty-four hours. So, we don't have to be back until tomorrow morning."

I can tell, he likes the idea of us having the entire night to ourselves.

"Is there anything else you had on our to-do list?" he asks.

I don't break his gaze as I simply shake my head no.

Beneath the table, I feel his hand come to my knee.

The touch is intimate, yet tender. It's cautious and unsure.

"So where do we go from here, Serena?" His tone drops low, husky. It sends shivers rolling down my spine, all the way to my lower belly.

I lean in just a little closer. I place my hand over his.

"I've been a good soldier my entire life," I say as I stare at his lips. "I've never stepped out of line. I've never done anything to put my unit in danger. I've never intentionally put myself in the line of danger that I didn't think I could get out of."

I trace my fingers over the contours of his hand, then slowly follow one prominent vein up over his wrist, to his forearm.

"I know what I should be doing," I confess. "But I just can't." My eyes rise back up to his from beneath my black eyelashes.

Jaxon studies me for a long moment. I make them count. I ground myself in the present. I burn how his hand feels on my leg into my memory. I memorize the way his eyes look. I embed the feeling of his heat radiating against my body.

"There has to be something in me that's stronger than the ultralight instincts," Jaxon says. "Serena, I just can't ever imagine trying to hurt you, not being able to fight it."

I look at him, and my heart breaks just a little bit. "Don't make me any promises. Not until you know. Until you feel it."

He leans forward and reaches up, cupping his hand to the back of my neck. He touches his forehead to mine. "It's not fair, Serena," he whispers. "I've just found you. So I'll just pray, with everything I have in me, that I'm stronger than you think I'll be."

I look up at him, meeting his eyes. We're so close. I can feel his breath on my lips. His nose brushes mine. I swear I can see into his eyes, all the way down to his soul that is speeding toward manifesting with every passing moment.

"One last night," I say in a breath. "It's all we've got. So let's make it count."

I love the smile that pulls on his lips. It's full of hope and excitement and mischief. "Let's make it count," he repeats. He slides toward the end of the bench and holds a hand out for me. "Come on. I've got an idea."

He drops a few bills on the table to cover the food and drinks we are never going to eat or drink. And he takes my hand in his, pulling me close as we quickly walk out of the restaurant.

"What was your last perfect night?" Jaxon asks as we push our way through the crowds.

"The night at the club," I spout off without hesitating.

Jaxon looks back at me with a mischievous grin. "The club is in the casino right next door."

I don't even try to hold back the smile that curls on my lips now. He doesn't have to say a word more.

We get back to the car and I pop the trunk. Jaxon starts digging through his bag.

I know exactly what I'm looking for. I grab the same red dress I wore the night we met.

I walk to the other side of the car, placing it between Jaxon and I. I look around to be sure no one is within eyesight, and I shimmy out of my pants. I wince a little as they brush over my fresh stitches. I pull my tank off. I step into the little red dress and zip it up the side.

Jaxon makes this…growling noise of approval and possession as I step back around. Unabashedly, his eyes run up and down my entire body. "Yes," is all he says, and all he has to say.

I keep staring at him as well, even as I pull on my black heels. He's wearing well-fitted black pants and a black button up shirt with the sleeves rolled up to his elbows, and the buttons up the front only done halfway up his chest.

I bite my lower lip as I let my imagination run wild.

A small, needy noise escapes my lips when he smirks and closes the trunk. He holds his hand out for mine, and we set off through the parking garage.

It takes us twenty minutes to work our way outside, next door, and then through the maze of the casino. The scent of smoke and alcohol is heavy in the air.

People are laughing and talking loudly and having a good time.

But my entire body is humming with awareness, focused solely on Jaxon next to me. His hand in mine. His body as it brushes against mine as we weave our way to our destination.

And finally, there is the sign for it, glowing in neon green.

I expect to step into the end of the line and wait our turn. There are at least twenty people waiting to get inside.

But Jaxon just walks straight to the bouncer. They obviously know one another, because the man just waves the two of us in.

I have to wonder, just how far is the Gray family's reach?

We step inside, into the dark hallway that leads into the heart of the club. The neon lights cast Jaxon in an unearthly glow, accentuating every one of his sharp features.

He looks like a dark god.

I just smile more.

The club is busy. It's already packed, and the night is only just beginning. The bar is full, and there are at least two hundred bodies on the floor.

Jaxon weaves his way through the crowd, confidently, guiding me and never once letting go of my hand.

And as we reach the very center of the room, he pulls me forward, turning me under his arm. He drops me back into a deep dip, supporting me by the back of the neck, his other hand gripping firmly on my hip.

I let my eyes slide closed and relish in every point of contact.

Jaxon drops his face, and slowly, he trails the tip of his nose from the base of my sternum, up between my breasts, and then up the side of neck as he slowly raises me back up to my feet.

I meet his eyes as I stand straight once again. I bring my right hand up to the side of his neck. And I let the music slowly sway my hips.

Jaxon takes a step forward, leading me backward. His hands come to my hips and his eyes fix on mine. The rhythm of the song is slow and sultry. I sway my hips again, Jaxon's hands tracking every single movement they make.

As we move, the crowd backs away, just enough to give us our space to move. Jaxon tracks his feet forward again, and I follow his lead, my body aligning with his perfectly.

I love to dance. I told him that the very first night we met.

This isn't what most of the other couples around us are doing. They're bouncing in time with the music. They're laughing and looking ridiculous in the name of fun.

This isn't for fun. What is happening between Jaxon and I is serious. It's a last night. A swan's cry before everything changes.

This has to be enough to last a lifetime. Because I've spent at least three lifetimes' worth being utterly miserable and lonely.

I finally found someone I don't feel lonely with. I finally found someone who aligns with my shadows. Someone who understands the danger my life is made of. I've finally found someone who doesn't look away from my monster form.

So this night, right here, right now, it has to count for everything.

As the song changes, I turn, my back to his front. Jaxon's hand slides from my hip, up slightly, covering my lower stomach, pulling me back in to him. His chest nestles into my back. I reach up, fisting my hands in his hair, and it falls loose from its tie.

He leans down, brushing his nose along the hollow beneath my ear. I feel his breath, hot and quick. It sends a wash of goosebumps flashing over my skin.

And then I feel his lips barely brush against my neck. Soft, gentle. Teasing.

My eyes slide closed as sparks ignite throughout my entire body.

Slowly, agonizingly slowly, Jaxon traces his fingertips from my wrists, down my forearms. He drags them down the sensitive underside of my upper arms. They brush their way down my sides, and then snake their way around my waist.

We're the perfect match. We align in every way. Dark with the dark. Scarred with the scarred. Bitter on bitter. Hope for hope.

Even our bodies were made to fit together. As we blend into one, I cannot imagine two people ever physically molding together better than Jaxon and I do.

I turn on the next song, placing one hand on his chest, on his bare skin where his shirt has been pushed aside, my other hand hooked behind his neck.

I stare at him. I breathe this moment in.

Jaxon's gaze could melt me through the center of the earth. In his eyes, I see everything. I have no doubt. He's feeling everything I am. He's feeling all of this. The good, the bad, the ecstasy and the agonizing truth that is coming for us.

He leans forward, touching his forehead to mine. My heart is thundering in my chest. It's racing so fast I feel like I'm going to die if something *more* doesn't happen, now.

And he grants me my wish. Slowly, his eyes slide closed, and he leans closer.

Closer.

I feel the heat from his lips.

My entire body finally calms in preparation for what I've secretly been dreaming about since the first time we met here.

We're practically glued to one another, so when his phone vibrates in his pocket, I feel it very clearly.

Jaxon freezes. I feel his internal debate.

This is ruining the perfect moment.

Does he ignore it?

But there is very, very little either of us can ignore in our lives.

He closes his eyes, his forehead still resting against mine, and he lets out a hard breath.

And I take just half a step back as he reaches into his pocket and pulls the phone out.

On the screen, I see Blake's name.

"I thought I'd made it pretty clear I need some space for a few days," Jaxon growls into the phone.

"Shut up and tell me the truth." Even though we're in a crowded, noisy club, my hearing is supernatural. I can clearly hear Blake's voice on the other end. "Did you up and join a cult or something?"

Jaxon's face screws up in confusion and annoyance. "What the hell are you talking about?"

"Two freaks just showed up here a few minutes ago, looking for you," Blake says. "They were dressed head to toe in all white. Seemed pretty determined to figure out where you are."

All of my insides go cold.

"And what did you tell them?" Jaxon growls as his eyes meet mine. He knows what this means.

"I told them that you'd run off with some chick you

just met," Blake says, sounding annoyed. "That you were long gone by now. Where did you say you were going?"

"North Dakota," Jaxon lies, thankfully recalling what he'd said earlier.

"Well, just thought you should know," Blake says. "You've got some real weirdos trying to find you. Have fun with your new queen of the dark."

Blake hangs up and Jaxon stares at the phone for just a second, still processing everything that was just said.

The Kindred. They're back. They're right here in Las Vegas again, still looking for Jaxon. Even after we killed the other one.

"I left my phone in the car," I say, realizing that if I'd had it with me, I either would have seen that they showed up on our systems, or the compound would have been calling me. I can only imagine how many missed calls I must have. "I should have seen them. I should have been more aware."

Jaxon grabs my upper arms. "It's okay," he says, but I can see in his eyes that he's worried. "Blake told them that we were leaving. They have no reason to think we're even around."

I've been too relaxed lately. I've been taking risks.

But when it comes to the Kindred, and when it comes to protecting Jaxon, I cannot gamble on assumptions.

I shake my head. "We can't take that risk," I say. "The Kindred will probably think Blake was lying. They're going to be suspicious because they've already fought three darklings, and we haven't released you. Because if you weren't the gatekeeper, we would have already released you."

Something shifts in his eyes, and I wonder if he's thought about it yet, that if he weren't what we were looking for, we already would have parted ways.

I'm so grateful we've found the gatekeeper.

But I'm far more grateful to have simply found *him*.

"We have to go back to the compound," I say, the fight seeping out of my voice. "We just can't risk it."

The expression falls on his face, and I can tell he wants to argue against it.

"Remember what it was like with that last one?" I ask. I reach up and touch the barely healed cut on his face. "It will be like that again. But now there are two of them."

Jaxon's hand raises and goes to the place where the ultralight burned me. His eyes study it, even though he can't see it.

I'm worried how they can hurt Jaxon, still entirely too human and barely able to defend himself.

He's thinking about the way that Kindred threw me around and nearly killed me.

"Okay," he says, his voice hoarse. "Let's go."

## Chapter Sixteen

Everything in me is breaking. It's cracking. Shattering. With every step we take out of the club, I find my throat getting tighter and tighter.

It was twelve perfect hours. There was an inquisition and stitches involved. A man was knocked unconscious and we witnessed an exorcism during those twelve hours.

But they were ours.

And we got these forty-five minutes in our club again.

But it's over now.

We step out of the club, and still hand in hand, we make our way through the casino. We step out onto the crowded sidewalk, the night fully descended now.

My legs feel stiff and full of lead as we walk down

the sidewalk to the building next door. Each of my feet feel as if they weigh two hundred pounds as we walk up into the parking garage.

And my stomach clenches in absolute dread when my car comes into view.

I stop fifteen feet from it, pulling Jaxon to a stop with me.

He looks back in anticipation, waiting for me to say whatever is on my mind.

I can't. I can't do this.

It's just not fair.

After 158 years of being angry and alone and resentful, now it's all different.

I've changed.

My eyes rise up to meet Jaxon's, and my heart breaks.

"Please try," I say. My voice comes out slightly strangled. I feel emotions biting at the backs of my eyes. "Don't...I don't want you making promises. But...just...please try."

The shift in his eyes breaks me further. I see the same agony in his eyes, the same cry of injustice.

He shakes his head, and he pulls me closer. "I'm yours, Serena," he breathes as he looks down at me. "It has to be enough."

Everything in me surges. I feel a rush of adrenaline. I feel my soul—my darkling—reach out, and attach itself to him, no matter what form he is in.

I rise up onto the balls of my feet, just at the same time Jaxon brings his hands to either side of my face.

And our lips crush together.

This kiss is desperate. It's full of anticipation and longing. It's claiming and possessive.

His lips are soft and his facial hair rough. It's bliss.

His mouth parts, an invitation I immediately accept. The breath shifts out of him and into me. I gasp, unable to get enough, unable to get my fill.

Jaxon's hands grow possessive. He pulls me closer, closer, only there is no more room between us. But somehow there is still too much.

Like wild vines growing in the forest, I feel our souls tangling together, spinning tighter and tighter. Me bound to him, him to me.

We can do this.

Somehow, we will overcome.

We will defeat the laws of the verse.

A moan escapes my mouth as I deepen the kiss. Jaxon's thumb brushes over my cheek and his other hand slides down my lower back, over my rear end as he pulls me closer and closer.

If I could freeze time, I would. I would spend the rest of eternity in this parking garage, my lips fixed on Jaxon's, our hands going everywhere need drives them.

I'm done. Ruined.

There will never be anyone else.

I belong solely to Jaxon Gray now.

He possesses my heart and my soul.

The heat inside of me builds, pushing the kiss deeper, stronger, longer.

Jaxon's hand on my lower back is strong. Warm.

His hand on my cheek is hot and possessive.

His lips are a raging inferno, gaining heat by the moment.

Another needy moan escapes my mouth. It's too much. It's not enough. The heat is exquisite.

Until suddenly my back is burning. My lips feel singed.

It's a reaction I don't have any control over.

My shadows slither out, billowing out around me, and lancing over every point of connection between Jaxon and I.

I stumble back a step and my eyes fly open.

"Serena," Jaxon says in a terrified breath.

I can see the heat radiating from his hands, but they're lanced with black scorch marks, almost as if he were struck by lightning. And the tips of his fingers are glowing a brilliant white.

In horror, my eyes rise to meet his. Only they stop at his lips, which have those same black scorch marks, as if he were struck by the darkness.

As if my shadows struck him, protecting me.

From an ultralight.

"Your lips," Jaxon says in horror as he takes a step

forward. He raises a hand instinctively, only he stops when he sees how his hand is glowing and radiating heat.

I step up to the car and look at my reflection in the window.

My lips are burned.

Just like the mark on my side, when the ultralight tried to kill me.

"Shit," Jaxon breathes as he walks up behind me. "That…that was me, wasn't it?"

I look back, following his line of sight, and then turn, looking at my reflection in the window.

There is a perfect handprint burned through the back of my dress, on my lower back, right where Jaxon's hand had been.

The tears finally well in my eyes. I stare at Jaxon, and I shake my head.

I am not ready.

I am not ready for this, however short it has been, to end.

But his hands are slowly, very slowly, beginning to burn brighter.

"We have to go," I say, just as the first tear breaks free. My insides are quivering. I feel like I might actually break apart and fall to the concrete at my feet in a million tiny shards. "We have to get you back to the compound."

Jaxon shakes his head. "Serena…"

"Don't," I say in a hoarse whisper that is barely loud enough to be heard. "There's nothing more we can do about it."

"How long?" he asks, even as the defeat takes over his shoulders, creeps into his eyes.

I shake my head. "I don't know. Minutes. An hour. I've never been this close when the manifestation happens."

Even now, he gives a hiss, stretching his neck out, as if there were a painful pinch in his chest. He reaches for the back of his shirt and pulls it up and over his head.

It falls to the ground in burned tatters.

With terror, he looks up at me.

"Get in," I say in a hurried hiss. "We have to get out of here."

He doesn't fight me now.

We both scramble into the car. I start it and throw it into reverse, flying out of our parking space. Like a maniac, I throw it into drive, and peel out as I point to the exit.

I don't even stop when I get to the main street. I simply get lucky that there are no bodies and no cars in my way.

I weave my way through traffic, crossing lanes, pulling into the opposite direction of traffic to hurry faster.

The engine revs, and my knuckles grow white on the steering wheel.

If Jaxon is worried about my reckless driving, he doesn't show it.

He pushes himself back against his seat, hard. His breath is coming out in hurried, harsh pulls, in and out.

I lay on the gas harder.

"I know we promised not to lock you up," I say, my voice growing frantic. "But what's about to happen… it's dangerous for everyone. You might kill us all without even lifting a finger. The vault was designed to withstand the manifestation. So—"

"Get me there faster," Jaxon huffs in a gruff voice, even as the temperature in the car rises.

What normally would take me fifteen minutes to get out of the heart of the city and onto the highway that leads out to the desert, takes me five.

I'm breaking every single traffic violation in the book. But every second matters, and I feel them burning up with every rise in temperature Jaxon is causing in the car.

Franticly, I search for my phone. I find it in the cup holder. I swear when I look down at the screen and see I have eighteen missed calls and thirty-two text messages.

I dial Davorian. He answers before it even begins ringing.

"There are two Kindred in Vegas," he instantly snaps into the phone. "Get back here, now!"

"I know," I hiss. "Get the vault ready though. It's happening."

Davorian goes quiet for a moment. This wasn't what he was expecting. "Now?"

I glance over at Jaxon. He's staring at his hands. His palms are now fully white. Energy dances on the surface of them, not quite flames, but far more than light or heat. "Right now."

"How far out are you?" he asks. I hear him get up from a seat and in the background, I hear him begin barking orders at the others.

"Twenty-five minutes," I say.

"We'll be ready," he says, and I hang up.

It should take me fifty minutes to get to the compound from here. But I might only have five until Jaxon fully manifests, and then it will be too late.

"Shit, why is it so hot in here?" Jaxon hisses as he pushes further back into his seat. I can see the heat radiating off of his chest now, his arms.

"Hold it in," I say, feeling desperate. I blast the AC as hard as it will go. "Just hold it in."

He breathes harder, his breaths feral huffs of air. His jaw is clenched tight, all of the tendons in his neck straining hard.

I take the last turn onto the dark highway, and fully lay on the gas.

"I have to be honest," he says through gritted teeth. "I was never really convinced that I was what you said I would be. You showed me what you are, I saw those three ultralights. But I never fully believed it was going to happen to me."

He suddenly lets out a howling yell, throwing his head back in pain.

He's burning with light from the inside out right now.

"Just hold it in a little longer!" I bellow as I look down and see the speed gage. I'm pushing 125 miles per hour.

If we were to pass a cop, we'd be long gone before they could get on the road and come after us.

Second by second, the temperature in the car is rising. Sweat beads on my forehead and my upper lip. I feel it drip down the center of my back. Even with the AC blasting, it feels like it has to be a hundred degrees in here.

The light emitting from Jaxon's hands is blinding by the time I pull off the highway and begin flying over the dirt road. I squint against it, feeling half blinded by it.

"Serena!" Jaxon yells in agony as he looks down at his hands.

The light creeps from his palms, up his wrists, a third of the way up his forearms.

"Hold it in!" I call as I press harder on the gas.

It's a rough, bouncy jaunt over the uneven ground once the dirt road ends. We climb in elevation and curl around rocky outcroppings.

And then finally, I see the split in the rocks.

I slam on the breaks, and barely get the car into park before we both explode from the car.

I shift mid-step. I grab Jaxon round the middle as I plummet down into the tunnel.

A roar of agony rips from my jaw as he burns me.

We tumble out of the tunnel in a roll, me shifting as we hit the floor.

"Hurry!" Davorian says.

They're all standing here, waiting at the entrance of the tunnel. Even the six new darklings who have returned from their stations. And every one of them looks at Jaxon with fear when they see his hands and arms glowing, feel the intense heat radiating off of him.

Jaxon glances at me with fear, but I just nod. And we take off running down the hallway.

With every step, more of Jaxon glows. The light is up to his elbows. I watch as his shoes completely burn off of his feat, the light creeping up his ankles. The temperature is sweltering.

At the end of the hall, Ascelin waits, holding the door open.

We've never used this room. We designed it so

many years ago, back in the sixties. It's built of solid steel, with a window twelve inches thick. It's the most unbreakable room we could come up with, that the best engineers at the time could come up with.

We've never known if it would be enough to contain an ultralight.

But we needed a place to contain the gatekeeper if we ever found them.

And now is the time to test it.

We slow as we run up to the door. And at the threshold, Jaxon turns, looking back at me.

His shoulders and chest are glowing. Blue flames are creeping up his hands. His neck and face have this glimmering white look, as if the light inside of him is ready to burst out.

My heart is thundering with fear.

I'm not a fearful person. But I am looking at an ultralight. The beings who have hunted us down, one by one, over the last century and a half. They've killed five hundred of us.

But this is Jaxon. This is my equal. The bearer of my heart.

And now it's here.

He's about to become the thing that hates me most.

I simply give a nod, even as one more tear streaks down my face.

"I'm yours, Serena," Jaxon says. His voice is so

rough, and it rings with the sonic tone of an ultralight. "It has to be enough."

More tears slip down my face. My lower lip is quivering, so I bite down on it. I can't find my voice. So, I simply nod, and wrap my arms around myself so I don't shatter to pieces.

With another desperate look, Jaxon turns, and steps inside the vault.

Ascelin closes it behind Jaxon, locking it with the most complex set of locks I've ever seen on this planet.

And the second it's locked, he turns. His dark eyes are cast on me, a look of anger and disgust on his face.

He grabs the front of my dress and backs me up in ten quick steps before I have a second to react. The others yell after him, but Ascelin stops when he plants my back against the glass wall of Nisha's office.

"What the hell do you think you are doing?" he hisses in a low voice, right in my face. "Running off with him? Letting him put his hands on you? What is *wrong* with you, Serena?"

I shake my head, wondering how he could possibly know.

But then my hand rises to my lips.

He saw the burn.

And the perfect handprint burned through my dress, all the way down to the skin of my lower back.

"Why?" Ascelin barks, loud and aggressive, right in my face.

The others stand back, watching, but none of them intervene. They can see the evidence of what me and Jaxon did, right on my face, just as easily as Ascelin can. They saw it on Jaxon's lips, as well.

"We don't always get to choose who we fall for," I answer quietly as I look away from them all.

"You went and fell for an ultralight?" Ascelin roars as he snaps me back against the glass once more. "That's like a spider falling in love with a butterfly. They're both arthropods, but the entire universe knows they don't belong together."

My blood chills, because he's drawn the perfect analogy.

"It doesn't matter anyway," I say, my voice sounding hollow. "Because in just a few minutes, it will all be over. And he'll never want to touch me again."

I see complex pain and anger on Ascelin's face, both warring for control.

He's hoped. I've never given him any reason to hope.

But he has.

And now I've gone and fallen for the worst person possible.

"This is dangerous, Serena," Philomena says. "Not just for you. For all of us."

My eyes shift to Davorian. "I never should have given you permission to leave this morning," he says in a quiet tone.

It astounds me that it was only this morning that we left. It feels as if weeks have passed. "Today wouldn't have changed anything," I admit. "It's been too late for a while."

The room goes ice cold with my admission.

Ascelin roars, snapping me back against the glass one more time before he turns away from me in disgust.

"While you've been hopping into bed with an ultralight, we've been tracking down the Kindred," he says through gritted teeth. "They were a mere two blocks away from you, Serena. They could have found you. They could have killed you. They could have taken the gatekeeper and then we'd all be stuck here for another century." He looks back at me over his shoulder. "Lucky for you, another ultralight has begun manifesting."

My eyes widen and my head whips around to look at the screens. "Where?"

Some of the tension breaks as the attention shifts. They all walk to the screens that show us the location of every ultralight in the LightVerse.

"Near Seattle," Nisha says, even as my eyes are drawn to that spot.

Jaxon is still glowing, brilliant and white, on the screen. But now there is another dot glowing just as bright, over a thousand miles northwest of us.

"We didn't even notice at first," Renwick says. He

walks up to my side, crossing his arms over his huge chest. His presence is almost comforting. His body language tells me he doesn't feel as strongly about what I've done as the others. "We were trying to track the Kindred in relation to your location. But suddenly they got on the road and hit the freeway. They're tracking toward the new ultralight."

"Well, I guess at least one thing is working in our favor today," I say. I lift my head. I roll my shoulders back.

No.

I'm not going to be ashamed. I'm not going to apologize for the way I feel.

I've felt good for the first time in years. I deserve to feel alive.

Maybe it's an impossible road before us.

And maybe it's already too late.

But I'm going to claim it.

I'm here until the end is sure.

I turn and face the others.

"I know you're all disgusted with me right now," I say. I know how I look. My lips burned, my dress singed. I know they could see the black scorches on Jaxon's face. "And I don't blame you. I would have felt the same way just a few weeks ago."

My eyes wander down the space, to where Jaxon's vault lies just beyond my line of sight.

"I never meant for it to happen," I say. "We met

before I knew what he was, and we had just one night together. Just an hour. But it was enough. It started the spiral that I couldn't stop."

I look up at Philomena. She thinks this is cut and dried. But her being with Renwick would have gotten her expelled from the academy back home.

I look at Renwick. I can see it in his eyes, he's not going to condemn me.

I glance at Nisha. She's as cold and flat as ever.

Ascelin's look of disgust and hatred hasn't softened.

So, I look to Davorian.

He doesn't seem to know how he feels. I see sympathy there. But also distrust. And also envy. In equal measures, there's disappointment.

"I don't apologize for what I've done," I say, lifting my chin just a bit. "I've fallen for an ultralight. And the past nine days might be all we get. But it was still worth it. I'll deal with whatever comes next."

Without another word, I walk back down the hall, past all of them. I aim for the vault.

With each step I take, the knot in my throat gets bigger. With every step I take, my stomach sinks a little farther.

I know how this ends.

I remember my own instincts.

I know how strong they are.

It's dangerous for us to just keep Jaxon here.

It's far more dangerous for my heart to hold on to hope.

I step down the hall, and finally, step into view of the vault.

Jaxon is crouched down, on one knee. His head is lowered. He's hunched in on himself, making him small.

But I watch as the flames consume more and more of his body. In a matter of a few seconds, while I stand here and watch him, his entire body is engulfed in flames.

He is shining so brilliant, I can barely stand to look at him.

The heat radiates off of him in waves that I can clearly see.

I'm breaking. I'm shattering.

Jaxon holds my heart and my soul. I gave it away during that kiss.

But here I watch him burn. As if he's burning through every ounce of my soul I've given him.

"A spider," Ascelin says with a sneer as the others walk up behind me, watching as well, as Jaxon finishes his manifestation. "And a butterfly."

Harder, harder, faster, faster, my heart thunders.

My palms are sweating.

All of my organs are trembling.

And once more, moisture wells in my eyes.

Fully engulfed in flames and light, Jaxon slowly rises to his feet. He curls up, one vertebra at a time.

As he rises to his full height, he opens his white, glowing eyes, staring straight at me. And his entire body bursts into sonic light.

## THE END OF BOOK ONE

# About the Author

Keary Taylor is the USA TODAY bestselling author of over thirty fantasy and science fiction titles. She grew up along the foothills of the Rocky Mountains where, from a young age, she started creating imaginary worlds and daring characters who always fell in love. She now lives on a tiny island in the Pacific Northwest with her husband and their two children. She continues to have an overactive imagination that frequently keeps her up at night.

facebook.com/kearytaylor

instagram.com/authorkearytaylor